EDGE OF PERIL

Fog Lake Mysteries

CHRISTY BARRITT

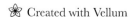

Complete Book List

Squeaky Clean Mysteries:

#1 Hazardous Duty

#2 Suspicious Minds

#2.5 It Came Upon a Midnight Crime (novella)

#3 Organized Grime

#4 Dirty Deeds

#5 The Scum of All Fears

#6 To Love, Honor and Perish

#7 Mucky Streak

#8 Foul Play

#9 Broom & Gloom

#10 Dust and Obey

#11 Thrill Squeaker

#11.5 Swept Away (novella)

#12 Cunning Attractions

#13 Cold Case: Clean Getaway

#14 Cold Case: Clean Sweep

While You Were Sweeping, A Riley Thomas Spinoff

The Sierra Files:
#1 Pounced
#2 Hunted
#3 Pranced
#4 Rattled
#5 Caged (coming soon)

The Gabby St. Claire Diaries (a Tween Mystery series):
The Curtain Call Caper
The Disappearing Dog Dilemma
The Bungled Bike Burglaries

The Worst Detective Ever
#1 Ready to Fumble
#2 Reign of Error
#3 Safety in Blunders
#4 Join the Flub
#5 Blooper Freak
#6 Flaw Abiding Citizen
#7 Gaffe Out Loud (coming soon)
#8 Joke and Dagger (coming soon)

Raven Remington
Relentless 1
Relentless 2 (coming soon)

Holly Anna Paladin Mysteries:

#1 Random Acts of Murder
#2 Random Acts of Deceit
#2.5 Random Acts of Scrooge
#3 Random Acts of Malice
#4 Random Acts of Greed
#5 Random Acts of Fraud
#6 Random Acts of Outrage
#7 Random Acts of Iniquity (coming soon)

Lantern Beach Mysteries

#1 Hidden Currents
#2 Flood Watch
#3 Storm Surge
#4 Dangerous Waters
#5 Perilous Riptide
#6 Deadly Undertow

Lantern Beach Romantic Suspense

Tides of Deception
Shadow of Intrigue
Storm of Doubt (coming soon)

Carolina Moon Series:

Home Before Dark
Gone By Dark
Wait Until Dark
Light the Dark
Taken By Dark

Suburban Sleuth Mysteries:
Death of the Couch Potato's Wife

Cape Thomas Series:
Dubiosity
Disillusioned
Distorted

Standalone Romantic Mystery:
The Good Girl

Suspense:
Imperfect
The Wrecking

Standalone Romantic-Suspense:
Keeping Guard
The Last Target
Race Against Time
Ricochet
Key Witness
Lifeline
High-Stakes Holiday Reunion
Desperate Measures
Hidden Agenda
Mountain Hideaway
Dark Harbor
Shadow of Suspicion
The Baby Assignment

Nonfiction:

Characters in the Kitchen

Changed: True Stories of Finding God through Christian Music (out of print)

The Novel in Me: The Beginner's Guide to Writing and Publishing a Novel (out of print)

Chapter One

THICK and pregnant with gray moisture, wisps of air played hide-and-seek with anyone caught in its mist.

As he stood on the rickety dock on the dark autumn evening, his breath blended with the fog—just as he blended with it—and he marveled at the sight. It was like he was one with the element, like it was part of him, like it bent to his will.

He breathed in and out. In and out. In and out.

The action was even, steady, and showed no nerves.

Probably because he wasn't nervous.

His big reveal was coming soon. Act One would begin, and the curtains to a person's worst nightmare would part, revealing him to his next victim.

He smiled at the thought of it, feeling like a kid at Christmas who was about to get just what he wanted.

As if on cue, the fog parted long enough for him

to see the lights in the window of the cabin in the distance.

Long enough for him to spot the woman inside.

Long enough for him to feel a pang of greedy hunger at what was to come.

The first time the hunger had staked claim on him, fear had pricked his skin and closed his throat. He had trouble coming to terms with what he had to do.

But, when he'd finished and seen his work, he'd never felt so . . . fulfilled.

So fulfilled that he wanted to do it again.

And so he had.

He hadn't been as nervous the second time.

And his hunger—his need for blood—had only grown stronger, more overwhelming and undeniable. It pressed on him with such potency that he couldn't ignore it.

Now he needed more to satisfy him. He was like an alcoholic desperate for another drink to numb his inner demons.

Or to feed them.

Except this time, he'd enjoy the process more.

He gripped the knife, repositioning his hands. The six-inch blade was sufficient. He'd sharpened it before he set out. The sharper, the better. Cleaner. Easier.

Flexing his fingers, he waited. The timing had to be just right. But all was well as the cool air invigorated his lungs—invigorated him.

In fact, the fog seemed to be in sync with his spirit.

The ebb and flow of the clouds couldn't have been orchestrated any better if he could control them. Its movement made everything feel shrouded with uncertainty.

With delight, he pictured how everything would play out. In a moment, he would make his presence known. When the woman saw him, her adrenaline would kick into high gear. She'd anticipate his arrival yet try to convince herself that she was safe. That her fear was silly. That she was imagining things. That there was no watcher in the mist, standing like a ghost from the past.

He smiled again.

She wasn't imagining things, though.

He took a step closer, the wood of the old dock groaning beneath his boots.

He was worse than a ghost.

He was real.

The fog rolled around him again.

Knife still gripped in his hand, he took another step.

Then he stood motionless.

And he stared.

He saw the woman again. She was sitting on her couch. Reading a book, maybe? She looked so peaceful and beautiful.

It was almost too bad.

But someone had to pay.

And, tonight, she was the chosen one.

He took out the bamboo cylinder from his pocket,

put it to his lips, and blew. The eerie sound of the Native American flute filled the air like a sad melody before death. The tune he played was well-rehearsed, and it was haunting—haunting enough to scare anyone.

It was his war cry.

He continued to blow into the pipe. To watch.

As the fog cleared, the woman looked up, finally hearing his song.

Her eyes widened.

Satisfaction pooled inside him.

She'd spotted him.

Fear ran through her gaze.

Now she was on guard.

Maybe she'd try to call 911.

Go ahead. It wouldn't matter.

As the fog covered him again, he swiftly walked toward the door.

Now was the time for the real fun to begin.

Chapter Two
_____

SHERIFF LUKE WILDER paused at the door of the small rental cabin.

James Cruise, his deputy, hurried past him and barely made it outside before he lost his breakfast on the patchy grass by the front porch.

The poor guy hadn't signed up for this. When Cruise became a sheriff's deputy, no doubt he'd expected to handle noise complaints, parking violations, and the occasional drug-related incident. That was usually the extent of the criminal activity around here at Fog Lake, Tennessee.

But not anymore. Not with three dead bodies in less than five months.

Luke wasn't ready to step inside the lakefront log home yet. No, he was still assessing the scene. And there was no hurry.

Their victim wasn't going anywhere.

She lay in the center of the kitchen, blood pooling on the knotty pine around her.

Luke waited until Cruise finished vomiting. Waited until the deputy straightened, wiped his mouth, and a moment of dignity had returned to his gaze.

"Tell me what you know," Luke said, his voice even and calm—a trait that frustrated anyone who'd ever wanted to get a reaction out of him.

"Yes, sir. Yes, Sheriff." Cruise wiped his mouth again.

The kid was only twenty-one, but he seemed younger. Maybe it was because Luke had known him since he was a baby. Maybe it was his shorter build and skinny stature.

But Luke couldn't figure out for the life of him why his father, the former sheriff, had hired this boy. Cruise was a good kid, yes. And he was from a good family. But that didn't mean he was cut out to be a cop.

"Go on," Luke said, waiting for Cruise to start. His deputy looked like he was fighting nausea again, like he was willing himself not to puke.

"I got the call at seven this morning," Cruise started, wiping his mouth with the edge of his sleeve again. "Larry Wheeler, the maintenance man with Axton Management Company, noticed that the door to this place had been open all morning. He was out here doing landscaping work. As he walked toward the house to check on things, he glanced inside and saw this woman on the floor. When he stepped closer, Larry knew it was too late—that she was dead—and he called the station."

"Did Larry come inside and disturb the crime scene?"

"No, sir."

"Where's Larry now? I'll need to talk to him."

"He's sitting in his truck. I told him we'd need a statement."

"Did you call the management agency yet to find out who was staying here?"

"No, sir. I just called you."

"Good job, Cruise. Why don't you go to your car, get yourself together, and make that call for me? I'll check things out here." Luke would also need to call in the TBI—Tennessee Bureau of Investigation. He hated to do it. He preferred to do things his own way.

But right now, these crimes were bigger than the three people in his small sheriff's department could handle. To not call would be irresponsible.

Luke glanced around the outside perimeter and didn't see anyone else near the cabin gawking or speculating about the presence of two sheriff's vehicles. That was good. Because the town's gossip chain would start soon enough. The more work Luke could do before he started fielding questions, the better.

As Luke slipped paper booties over his shoes, he stared through the doorway. He already had a good idea of what to expect when he stepped inside. But he needed to rid himself of any bias. Every scene required an open mind. Every scene *deserved* an open mind.

But, as Luke moved into the crime scene, the stench inside swept him back in time.

Blood. The metallic, rotting odor transported him back to his days as a detective in Atlanta. Took him back to the Rocky Ridge murders. The string of deaths had nearly been his undoing.

Luke glanced down at the woman on the floor.

Just as he suspected, she was a brunette. Slender. In her twenties. Pretty. Just like the last two victims.

He would guess she was staying here alone.

Luke would also guess that she'd been killed by a single cut across her neck.

There would be no sign of sexual assault or even a struggle. No, it was like a ghost had stepped inside the house, sliced her throat, and disappeared.

Of course, Luke would only think those things if he began making assumptions again.

Which he wouldn't do.

As he peered at her face, he sucked in a quick breath.

Just as he suspected—the victim's blood had been smeared in small circles across her cheeks, almost making her look like a doll.

It was the killer's calling card, so to speak.

This town needed a lot of prayers right now. Once word of this leaked out, the tourists would be running far away from here.

And the town's livelihood would die.

Again.

Harper Jennings parked her ten-year-old sedan on the street and climbed out. As she slammed her door, her rearview mirror fell to the dashboard, and she sighed.

She'd tried to have it fixed three times now, and nothing seemed to work. Couldn't she ever catch a break?

She'd deal with that later.

Right now, she paused.

A cool fall breeze enveloped her, and she drew in a deep breath of fresh mountain air. This couldn't be the right place. Fog Lake looked like a forgotten Mayberry, not like the setting of a real-life slasher movie.

In its heyday, this town had probably been extraordinary. It had all the right bones in place.

Main Street, where she stood, had plenty of frontage, and rustic signs boasted of businesses new and old. A movie theater advertised one film with one showing per day. The standard hardware store, diner, restaurant, gift shop, and art gallery all stood within sight.

In the spirit of October, pumpkins and haybales had been placed on corners. A banner across the street proclaimed an invite to the upcoming Fog and Hog Festival. *Fog and Hog?* It sounded interesting.

All around the town, the Smoky Mountains rose

up like a mighty fortress. Clouds rimmed the tops of the autumn-drenched peaks. And, somewhere in the distance, the lake stretched out like a body about to be put to rest.

The beautiful lake that was always draped with fog. With mystery. Romance. Intrigue. Online articles called it "atmospheric."

It was almost perfect here.

As the thought rolled through her mind, Harper sucked in a long breath.

Except it wasn't.

She knew every place had its secrets. But this town seemed to be brimming with them. The constant fog surrounding the place almost seemed like an overflow of sin from the town's underbelly.

A shiver raked down her spine at the mental image.

Maybe she shouldn't have come here. Harper still had nightmares about the events that began eight years ago. Even on a good night, she could hardly sleep. Every creak awakened her. Her dreams were tormented, like an unseen force drove them into a valley of madness, and she was unable to steer them back into peaceful territory.

Every. Single. Night.

Yet Harper had no choice but to come to Fog Lake.

As a crowd passed on the sidewalk, most wearing jeans, flannel shirts, and boots, Harper glanced down. She probably should have changed before she came here. She was definitely overdressed for the outdoorsy community in her black pencil skirt, heels, and button-up blouse.

But Harper hadn't had time to change. When she'd heard about the newest murder victim, she'd told her boss she had to take some vacation time, and she'd left right then. She hadn't even been sure her old clunker of a car would make the nine-hour trip from DC. It didn't matter. She was determined to get here, even if she had to walk.

What she didn't know was how her presence here would be received. How people would react to her story. If she was wise to walk into a killer's den like this.

She rubbed the scar at her throat, carefully concealed by her blouse.

You can do this. You have to try, at least. Make them listen.

That was right. Harper had no choice but to share what she knew. She had to do this. The conviction inside couldn't be ignored.

Her mom had always told Harper that her conviction would one day be her downfall.

Maybe her mom was right.

Swallowing hard, Harper hiked her purse up on her shoulder and started toward the sidewalk. Her heels clacked against ground accustomed to hiking boots and adventure seekers—not struggling reporters having a career crisis.

After searching the signage, Harper found the place she was looking for.

The sheriff's department.

Drawing in one more deep breath, she pulled the glass door open and saw a frenzy of activity inside. The air seemed to buzz with adrenaline.

No one noticed Harper, so she stood there a moment, watching everything almost as if invisible. These weren't just sheriff's deputies. No, other people had been called in. The Tennessee Bureau of Investigation, if she had to guess.

A petite, frail-looking woman finally paused and squinted up at Harper. "Can I help you?"

Harper licked her lips and glanced at the woman who wore her gray hair in a bun and held a clipboard close to her chest. "I'm looking for the sheriff."

The woman hugged her clipboard tighter and frowned. "I'm afraid he's busy right now. Is it an emergency?"

"I don't know." Harper nibbled on her bottom lip, knowing how her words sounded. It wasn't that she doubted herself. The urging in her gut was too strong to ignore. But Harper felt pulled in two different directions. Stay and be mocked? Run and be safe?

Any sane person would run and forget about all of this.

The woman didn't look perturbed at Harper's words. Instead, she offered a gentle, motherly smile. "Well, is it life-or-death? Let's start there."

Here goes nothing. "I think I know who's responsible for the murders in this town, and I'd like to speak with the sheriff about it. I drove all the way here from DC. It can't wait."

The woman's eyes widened, and she took a step back, as if Harper's words had spooked her into action. "Let me see if I can find him for you, then. Wait right here."

Harper crossed her arms and nodded.

And then she prayed she was doing the right thing. She prayed long and hard.

But the fact remained that almost everyone in her life had let her down. And that meant she didn't have much left to lose.

Chapter Three

LUKE SAT at his desk and stared at the information he'd put together on the murder victim they'd found yesterday morning.

Amy Mintel. Twenty-six years old. From a small town outside of Nashville. Single.

According to her mother, Amy had come to Fog Lake to take pictures. She wanted to make a living as a photographer and was building her portfolio. Amy thought she was invincible, her mother said. She was the adventuresome type who liked to rock climb and hike and whitewater raft. She'd suffered from the naivete of youth.

Luke had ascertained that part. Only the young thought they were invincible.

Just like Luke had thought at one time. He figured that he had the whole world in front of him. Little did he know that things had been set in motion long ago to lead him back here today. He daily had to remind himself that the sacrifice was worth it. He hadn't seen any fruit of that yet, but he had to hold onto the hope that he would one day.

He rubbed his eyes as he stared at the file a little longer.

Yesterday, Amy's parents had gone to the medical examiner's office in Knoxville to ID their daughter's body. In a couple days, when the ME gave the okay, Amy would be taken home so she could be put to rest and family and friends could say goodbye.

There wasn't much more to examine. Amy had died from a knife wound to the throat. The blade had sliced her carotid artery, and she'd bled out. Her death had been quick.

And needless.

So needless.

A knock sounded at his door, and Luke looked up to see Ms. Mary standing there, peering at him with worry in her gaze. "Someone's here to see you. Claims she has information on the killer. Do you have a minute?"

Luke had already vetted twenty phone calls today with false leads, and three other people had come in claiming to have seen someone acting suspicious around town. None of those "leads" had panned out.

Most people had good intentions, but, in the end, their help had ended up being a waste of time—and time was a valuable commodity in investigations like this. The pressure in town was building, building . . .

and soon Fog Lake wouldn't be able to contain it—unless Luke could stop this madness in time.

"She drove here from DC," Ms. Mary continued.

DC? The trip wasn't something most people would do on a whim.

Luke let out a sigh, still feeling cautious and exhausted. Despite that, he said, "Send her in then. I'll hear her out."

He glanced out his doorway, beyond Ms. Mary, and saw that the TBI team was leaving. They'd checked out the crime scene, and now they would handle the forensic side of this investigation. Luke would handle the manpower here in Fog Lake and be in touch with the field office in Knoxville about any developments.

He hated to say it, but he was thankful the agents were leaving.

Luke preferred the quiet, preferred doing things his own way.

"Luke." Ms. Mary paused and wrung her hands together, delaying her departure.

"Yes, Ms. Mary?" She had taught Luke's Sunday school class during his elementary years so, even though she was officially his employee, she'd always be Ms. Mary to him. On occasion, she still liked to catch Luke off guard and ask him to recite the books of the Bible.

"Are we safe here?" Her voice cracked as the question left her lips. She was a widow, and she lived alone in a cabin up the road from Luke. She had reason to be scared.

Two murders people might be able to justify as a terrible tragedy. Three? It was a terrifying truth no one could deny.

Evil had come to their town.

A rock formed in his stomach. Luke couldn't lie to the woman. Yet not many people could handle the truth. "To be honest, I don't know if we're safe. I really don't know."

He leaned back in his seat—an old, worn desk chair with duct tape on the arms. A seat that had belonged to his father for thirty years. Luke couldn't bring himself to replace it.

But it always reminded him that he had big shoes to fill. Shoes he didn't want to fill. But a promise was a promise.

A moment later, Ms. Mary ushered a woman into his office and shut the door as she left.

Luke quickly observed the visitor's professional clothing. Designer handbag. Long, dark hair that was curly but neat.

Luke's guard went up. It wasn't that he didn't trust outsiders. It was that he didn't trust anyone. Not easily, at least.

He stood and extended his hand, keeping his tone professional as he said, "Sheriff Luke Wilder."

The woman's handshake was gentle but firm. "I'm Harper Jennings. I know you're busy, so thank you for seeing me."

She wasn't from this area. She didn't have the rolling accent of people here in these mountains. Luke would guess she was from the mid-Atlantic region, a place with a strange blend of Southern euphemisms and Northeastern briskness.

"What can I do for you, Ms. Jennings?" Luke nodded toward the seat on the other side of the desk.

She lowered herself there, swallowing hard as a hint of her inner turmoil showed through. "Sheriff, I don't know where to start, so I suppose I'll get right to the point. I heard about the murders here in town, and I think I know who's responsible."

This conversation just got a whole lot more interesting.

Or this woman was a kook, someone who came out during events like this, trying to get attention. He'd reserve his judgment.

He folded his hands together. "And who would that be?"

Harper stared at him a moment, an unknown emotion floating in her eyes—something that resembled doubt and a touch of fear. "I think my brother is behind the murders. His name is Billy Jennings."

Luke processed her words before slowly, carefully responding with, "And why do you think this?"

She rubbed the strap of the leather purse that rested on her lap. "He . . . well, he has some issues. I heard a few details about the case, and he fits the MO."

"The MO?" he repeated. Was this another case of

someone who'd watched too many episodes of *Law and Order*?

He'd seen it before. Watch a few detective shows on TV, and suddenly people were experts.

Luke hated to be such a skeptic . . . but it usually paid to be cautious in the long run.

"My brother—he was adopted into our family out of the foster care system—and he . . . he liked to watch people," she continued.

"No crime in that."

"He also had a strange fascination with Native American instruments."

Luke absorbed that additional fact. Native American instruments? How did this woman know about that? They'd kept that detail from the 911 calls quiet.

He tempered his response. "And what do those have to do with the case, Ms. Jennings?"

"The first two victims heard a flute being played right before they died." She said the words matter-of-factly, not in a "gotcha!" fashion.

Luke's muscles clenched tighter and tighter. "What makes you think that?"

Harper frowned and rubbed her neck, right above her collar bone. "I talked to one of the victim's family, and they told me. Said their daughter called them right after calling the police. Said she'd seen a man in the fog and then heard someone playing this eerie Native American-sounding song on a flute or pipe of some sort."

Luke needed to rewind a bit here. "You randomly called a family of one of the victims?"

Her cheeks reddened. At least she had the decency to look embarrassed. "Look, how I found out isn't important. I need you to listen to me. Please."

Luke studied her another moment. She looked sincere. And nervous. And she'd come a long way to share this with him.

Still, something about her put him on edge. What was it?

Harper let out a sigh, a touch of her gusto disappearing until she finally shook her head, her countenance crestfallen. "And I know about the blood on the victim's cheeks."

That information definitely hadn't been leaked. No, all the townspeople knew was that three women had been murdered by knife with a slash across their throats.

He tried not to show a reaction, to indicate that she was right or wrong.

Her story was interesting, but it offered him nothing. It only proved that she had indeed talked to the victim's family and that they'd shared too much information.

Luke picked up his pen. "How about this? You give me your brother's contact information, and I'll see what I can find out."

Her head dropped and, when she looked back, agony stained her eyes. "There's one other thing."

"What's that?"

She licked her lips, the distress in her gaze growing by the moment. "Sheriff, my brother is dead."

———

Harper stared at the sheriff's face as he stared back, looking dumbfounded.

"Dead?" Sheriff Wilder repeated, shifting in his seat.

"That's what they say, at least." She held her breath, waiting for his reaction. She knew how this sounded. Knew she sounded crazy.

"What does that mean?"

Harper rubbed her throat again. "The police say he died in a car accident a year ago. His body was supposedly burned beyond recognition."

"And you don't think he actually died?"

"I'm just telling you that Billy Jennings has done all of the things that the killer in your town has done."

"I mean no disrespect, but when you say that, you mean he's watched people and he plays a Native American instrument." Skepticism tinged his voice.

After a moment of hesitation, Harper tugged down the collar of her shirt. "And he tried to do it to me also."

The sheriff's eyes widened as he studied the scar across her neck. She knew how it looked. Pinkish gray. Four inches. Thick.

"Billy did that?"

"I can't prove it. The police never caught the man responsible. But I know it was Billy."

"How do you know?"

"It happened after I moved out and I was on my own. I hadn't seen Billy in nearly five years. One night I woke up, and there he was staring at me, just like he had in the past. He had a knife in his hands."

"I see." The sheriff studied her another minute before slowly exhaling. "Let me see what I can find out, Ms. Jennings."

"Call me Harper. Please."

"Okay, Harper. I'll look into it. Are you staying in town?"

"I plan on getting a room at a local hotel."

"Try the Whistling Pines. It's one of the nicer ones. And give me your cell number before you go."

Relief filled her. The sheriff had sounded cordial, at least. Maybe Harper had gotten through to him. Maybe.

She'd been so afraid that no one would listen.

She followed his lead, standing and walking toward the door. But his demeanor had changed. He suddenly didn't seem as skeptical or weary. A new curiosity flickered in his gaze.

"I'll be in touch," he told her, gently touching her elbow. "Thank you for coming forward."

"Of course."

Harper left, fishing her keys from her purse as she walked to her car.

The sheriff had been younger than she expected.

For some reason, she'd pictured a man in his late fifties with a bushy beard and a gut. Sheriff Luke Wilder appeared to be in his early thirties, with a head full of dark hair, a square jaw, and a fit build.

But there was something else in his gaze. Some kind of sadness or heaviness that made her curious.

However, she had more important things to think about right now. Things like murder and stopping a serial killer.

Climbing back into her car, Harper drove through the downtown area and past a friendly looking town square until she reached the lake. There, on the left side, stood the Whistling Pines Motel.

She craned her neck up to see it for a moment. Here at Fog Lake, even the hotels looked like massive log cabins. It was part of the area's charm, she supposed. Harper hoped they had a vacancy.

After parking, she hurried into the lobby.

A woman behind the counter offered a brief half-smile at Harper when she walked in then turned back to the counter, where an older couple stood. Five suitcases surrounded them, and their tones were elevated.

"Now, there's no hurry to check out," the motel clerk said, her tone appeasing.

"We heard about the woman who died." The man ran a hand over his salt-and-pepper mustache. "We can't stay here any longer. I know this is quieter than Gatlinburg and Pigeon Forge. But we'll take the crowds over a murderer."

The clerk looked paler. "I understand."

As they continued with the early checkout process, Harper sensed someone beside her. Her muscles tightened.

Keep your cool, Harper. Keep your cool.

She glanced back and saw a man with red hair and greenish eyes standing there, watching the scene in the distance, just like she did.

"It's been a madhouse around here since word leaked about the murder," he told her.

"I can imagine."

"You look like you're checking in, though," he continued. "You look too polished to have been here in the mountains for any amount of time."

"Yeah, long story." The less people who knew the details, the better. People wouldn't respond well if they found out Harper thought her brother was behind the terror in this town. "You here to check out?"

"No, I'm here to get some more towels. I figure I'm safe. I'm with my friends, and I'm . . . well, I'm a male. Not to sound sexist. But the victims have all been women."

"I can't argue with that. What are you and your friends doing here in Fog Lake?" Harper may as well chat as she waited. At least it kept her mind occupied.

"Hiking. We come down from Cincinnati every year for a trip. I'm Ian, by the way. Ian Michaels."

"Harper." She took his hand and shook it. "Nice to meet you."

Just then, the couple brushed past with their fleet

of luggage, and the motel clerk motioned Harper forward.

"I'll see you around, Harper," Ian said, just as a maid stepped out with a stack of towels.

"See you." Harper pulled her suitcase toward the counter and offered the woman there a compassionate smile. "Crazy day?"

The clerk, whose nametag read Martha, was probably in her thirties, with thinning brown hair pulled back into a sloppy ponytail. She had a round face, free of makeup, and looked like she'd had better days.

Martha rolled her eyes. "Everyone's gone crazy. I'm sure you've heard what happened. Everyone has."

"Another dead body." Harper's throat tightened as she said the words.

"Yes, and everyone thinks they'll be next. This is supposed to be peak season around here, and the way it's looking, I'm going to come out in the hole. Not to mention that historically this is our busiest weekend with the upcoming festival."

"I'm sorry to hear that."

The woman waved her hand in the air. "Listen to me. Going in the hole will be my own doing if I keep talking like this. I'm the one scaring off guests now."

"You didn't scare me off. In fact, I'd like a room."

No, you should run, Harper. Go back to DC. Why would you ever stay here?

Her grandfather had always told her that courage wasn't the absence of fear, but the ability to face what scared you. She'd always held onto that nugget of wisdom. He'd died when she was only seven, and Harper had missed him ever since.

"Best news of the day. I'll give you the best one I have available, just for the fact that you're brave enough to stay."

"Well, this killer hasn't struck at a hotel yet anyway, right?" Harper had meant the words to be lighthearted, but she'd heard the twinge of her fear in her own voice.

"Exactly! I mean, that doesn't mean he won't." The woman's face tightened. "I shouldn't have said that either. Our rooms are very secure."

Her words didn't make Harper feel any better, but she said nothing.

The woman handed her a key. "Here you go. Like I said, one of the best rooms I have, with a great view."

She pulled out a map and showed Harper the location. Of course, it was on the top floor, at the corner, and outside. Probably one of the most secluded rooms here at the motel.

But that was okay.

As Martha finished the paperwork, Harper leaned casually against the front desk. "Any idea where this last crime happened?"

Martha glanced around before lowering her voice. "Not a hundred percent, but I heard it was at one of the cabins down at the end of Elk Row Lane."

"It is rather . . . spooky, isn't it?" Spooky was an

understatement. It was terrifying, and everyone in town knew it.

Harper glanced behind her and saw more people coming in—probably to check out early based on their frowns and heavy sighs.

"Everyone's losing their minds. You don't understand. We didn't have a murder here for fifty years, and now . . ."

"Someone's bent on changing that." The words caused Harper's throat to ache.

"Exactly. It doesn't make sense. Why would a killer come to a town as peaceful as this?"

That was a good question. Why had he chosen this place?

Harper still had so many questions. And she wasn't leaving here until she found some answers.

Chapter Four
_____

LUKE STAYED at his desk and reflected on what Harper Jennings had told him. It would take a while for what she said to sink in.

Before Harper arrived, Luke's leads in this case had been at zero.

Whoever this killer was, he'd aced the art of not leaving any evidence behind. No trace fibers. No fingerprints. No tread marks. Nothing on security footage.

Luke had spent the entire day yesterday interviewing Larry, the maintenance man, as well as the neighbors nearest to the crime scene and various people who had interacted with Amy while she was out and about in town.

No one had seen anything suspicious.

Just like with the first two murders.

It didn't seem right. This guy—the killer—hadn't just appeared out of thin air. Someone somewhere

had to have seen something. And then Harper
Jennings breezed into the chaos with her theory.

As Luke sat in the rickety office chair, he pictured
the woman. Her eyes contained an intelligence Luke
couldn't ignore. And she didn't appear to have a stake
in this investigation. Why would she have come
forward with that story if it wasn't true? What would
she possibly have to gain?

With no other ideas, Luke turned to his computer
and typed in the name and information Harper
Jennings had given him.

Billy Jennings. Twenty-four-years old. Light brown
hair. Slim build. Five feet ten inches.

Strange. He couldn't even find a record of the
man's death.

Luke stared at the screen another moment, trying
to plan his next move. Out of curiosity, he typed in
"Harper Jennings."

Pages and pages of results popped up.

He leaned back, ready to learn something new
about the mysterious stranger who'd shown up in
town with a theory and a scar across her neck.

As he scanned the first result, he released a long
breath. Harper was a political reporter with the *Wash-
ington Pilot*. Interesting.

So there went his theory that she didn't have a
stake in this. She could have made up the whole story
in an effort to get information from him. He'd seen
the tactics reporters used to get information for their

big break—their moment of fame as they were the first to catch wind of big news.

One of his past cases was ruined when a reporter leaked information she shouldn't have known. Luke's gut still churned as he thought about it. No, as far as Luke was concerned, journalists weren't to be trusted. They were the enemy.

Yet . . . that scar.

His thoughts remained conflicted.

On a whim, he picked up his phone. He found the number for Candace Jennings, Harper's mother. Luke knew it was a longshot, but he needed to put this so-called lead to rest. This was the only way he could think of to do that.

A woman with a high-pitched, well-enunciated voice answered on the first ring.

"I'm trying to reach Candace Jennings," Luke said, capping and uncapping the pen in his hands.

"Speaking. Who is this?"

"I'm Sheriff Luke Wilder of Fog Lake, Tennessee, and I'm calling in regard to your son, Billy Jennings."

"Billy?" Surprise tinged her voice. "What do you want to know about Billy?"

"I'm trying to verify he passed away in an auto accident a year ago."

"Yes. Of course. Why are you asking?"

"His name was brought up in an investigation."

She paused. "Wait, did Harper tell you to look into Billy?"

Luke straightened at the accusatory tone in the woman's voice. "Why would you ask that?"

"Because she's always starting trouble. Don't listen to a word she says. She just wants to bring Billy shame, even in death."

"She wants to bring her brother shame?" He leaned back and chewed on that statement.

"She always had it out for him. Let me guess—she told you she got that scar on her throat from him."

"You're saying she didn't?"

"She was the one in a car accident. I tell you what —you should stay away from her. You'll thank me later for warning you."

"Why's that?"

"Because she's trouble. Maybe she's the one you should be looking at."

With that, the line went dead.

Luke stared at his phone for a moment.

Interesting.

That conversation hadn't gone the way Luke had expected. And suddenly he felt like he was right back to zero with this investigation.

After Harper dropped her things off in her room, she decided to change into some jeans and then wander around town a bit. She'd never liked being alone in small spaces. Her apartment always felt like the walls were closing in.

She hadn't always been this way. Only since three years ago. Since Billy broke in.

Before leaving her room, Harper paused and glanced in the bathroom mirror. She flinched at the reflection.

Red circles stained her cheeks.

Red from her own blood.

Red that made her look like a doll—a demented doll.

She blinked, and the image changed.

The woman staring back looked normal. No red cheeks.

Just Harper with her curly hair, defined cheeks, and brown eyes.

Harper let out an airy laugh and squeezed her eyes shut.

She was just seeing things.

Again.

Billy hadn't marked her for life.

No, she'd been able to wash those red cheeks away. But the memory would always haunt her. Quickly, she splashed some cool water on her face and used a fluffy white towel to dry the moisture.

You can do this, Harper. You can do this.

She stepped outside, happy to leave her hotel room behind. Now that night had fallen, the cold air felt even more brisk. She shoved her hands into the pockets of her black leather jacket. The sleek coat didn't scream mountain living, but at least she had the flannel shirt to go with it.

She glanced down from her balcony at the glowing streets below. From here, she could see the town square, which was complete with a large wooden gazebo in the center of it. Shops lined the area, and the whole community sat nestled against the lake. Dotted around the mountainside and along the shore lights shone from cabins filled with tourists.

Usually, at least.

Maybe not right now.

She examined the mountains for a moment. Did they shield the town? Or did they trap the community within its guarded confines? After all, there was only one road that led in—and out. The thought was rather unnerving.

She'd always liked the mountains and small towns. DC was entirely too busy for her tastes. Even Raleigh had seemed too big for her when she was growing up. Her mom had told her she'd never make it in a small town, that they had nothing to offer.

Maybe one day Harper would find out for herself. Once she could afford to give up her steady paycheck. Making it on her own was harder than she'd ever imagined. But since her mother had disowned her, she truly had no one to fall back on.

As Harper glanced around, a shiver pinched her spine.

Why did she feel like someone was watching her?

The thought was ridiculous.

The only person who might be watching her was Billy, but he couldn't know she was here—not yet.

Yet Harper was certain Billy was here.

He hadn't followed his victims into town. He hadn't chosen his victims first. No, she was sure he'd chosen this place and then he'd found his victims here. Another shiver went down her spine.

Why, Billy? Why this town? What happened in your past to lead you here?

Harper had no idea.

"Hey, it's you again," a deep, playful voice said. "I guess we're neighbors."

She glanced over and saw Ian emerge from the door beside hers. "Hey, stranger."

He stood at the balcony with her. The town was to their right, and, at their left, lay the lake. Fog had already rolled out over the water, giving it a mystical quality.

"It's a beautiful sight, isn't it?" Ian asked.

"It's gorgeous. Too bad it's now tainted."

Ian reached out his hand as if trying to touch the air. "It is too bad. But I find this place fascinating, despite the murders. It's almost like the fog is alive, isn't it?"

As he said the words, the vapor seemed to mist over his hand. It was almost as if Ian were a magician with a mastery of special effects.

Harper sucked in a breath, realizing just how creepy the thought was. "Yeah, it is."

He dropped his hand, done with his theatrics. "I guess it's fitting that a town with such a tragic past is experiencing such a tragic future as well."

"Tragic past?"

His eyebrows knit together. "You didn't know?"

"Know what?"

"The history of this town, this lake? The massacre? It dates back to the Native Americans—"

"Hey, Ian! Come on. Let's go!" A group of three guys called from the parking lot. "Stop flirting."

He smiled sheepishly but didn't deny the accusation. "The story will have to wait until another time."

Harper bit back her disappointment. "I guess so."

That feeling returned to her—the feeling of being watched. She glanced down at the lake and sucked in a deep breath when she saw a man standing there. He watched her without shame.

Billy?

He looked the same age. Same build. Yet he hunched over, somehow appearing downcast, even from far away.

"That's Larry, the maintenance man," Ian said. "I wouldn't mind him. He's the quiet, mysterious type. I met him when the heat stopped working in my room, and he came in to fix it. He works most of the properties with the management company."

That didn't make Harper feel any better. Instead, she rubbed her throat, willing her muscles to loosen. "Good to know."

As his friends began heckling him again, Ian took a step away and paused. "Listen, we're headed down to a concert on Main Street tonight. It's a local band —Rosie and the Men Who Stole My Land. I know it doesn't sound PC, but it is. She's a Native American and her band is all white guys. Anyway, you should come."

"Maybe later," Harper told him. "Thanks for the invite."

But Harper had other more pressing things to do right now.

As she glanced back at the lake, she noticed that Larry was now gone.

The thought didn't comfort her.

Chapter Five

HARPER CLUNKED DOWN THE STAIRS, across the street, and stepped onto the sidewalk leading to the downtown area—which was bustling tonight. Sure enough, she heard music in the background. The band had an acoustic rock vibe, which had always been her favorite. Too bad she wasn't here for fun.

Harper scanned the people on the streets. Many were out having a good time—either oblivious to danger or not caring about it. But a few groups she saw walked fast, like they were here but anxious.

Why did that uncomfortable feeling remain? That feeling that a hunter was out there and had Harper in his crosshairs?

Maybe she shouldn't have come here.

But if someone else died . . . she'd feel responsible.

She had to stop this madness.

Harper glanced farther down the street and spotted a sign for the Hometown Diner. She could use a bite to eat. Plus, a diner would be a great place to listen to local scuttlebutt.

She walked inside, and it looked just as she'd imagined. A little bar stretched across the back wall, several booths nestled on the outside edges of the room, and everything looked nostalgically outdated. Overhead, Chubby Checker sang about doing the twist, and the smell of french fries and sizzling burger patties made her stomach growl.

It was perfect.

Harper found a seat at the corner of the bar toward the back, a place where she could keep an eye on everyone coming and going. After ordering a salad with grilled chicken, she turned to watch the people around her.

She'd just gotten started with her perusal when a woman sat in the open seat beside her. Harper could tell by the sparkle in her eyes and her ready smile that the woman was an extrovert.

Harper would guess the woman to be about her age—twenty-seven—give or take a few years. She had light brown hair and a curvy build that was only highlighted by the deep V of her red T-shirt.

"Hey, there," the woman started, grabbing a laminated menu.

"Good evening." Harper had hoped to watch people and listen to their conversations for a while longer before speaking with anyone. She was a processer. She observed. Formed opinions and plans. And then she proceeded.

But she wasn't going to pass up the opportunity to possibly find out more information about the town.

The woman distracted herself with the menu before ordering a burger, fries, and milkshake. Then she glanced back at Harper. "I met her once, you know."

Harper blinked in surprise. "Excuse me?"

"The woman who died. Her name was Amy."

"Oh . . . I see." That had been random, but not necessarily bad.

"Everyone's talking about her right now. I figured you were probably thinking about her also. Who isn't?"

Harper rested her elbows on the counter, realizing this conversation might be fortuitous. "Where did you meet her?"

"On a hiking trail. She was a photographer, and she'd come into town to take some photos. She wasn't full-time or anything. Said she was trying to build up her portfolio."

Interesting. The details of the case hadn't been released yet, so what Harper knew was scattered. "She came here alone?"

"She did. Said her boyfriend was supposed to come with her, but he got called away on a business trip at the last minute. She said work always took first priority for him. She didn't want to miss peak week, so she decided to come anyway. I'd say good for her, but . . ."

How would things have turned out differently if

Amy hadn't decided that? Harper bit down. She had no idea. But it was tragic the woman's trip had ended as it did. So, so tragic.

"Did she seem nice?" Harper asked. Not that it mattered. If Amy had been a jerk, she still wouldn't have deserved to die like that.

"She did seem nice. And she was pretty. That was the first thing I noticed about her. She had dark hair that was on the longer side. Kind of like you."

Harper touched the ends of her hair, strangely disturbed by the comment. "Are you a local?"

A smile cracked the woman's face. "Where are my manners? I'm Shirley Cue."

Shirley Cue? Since the woman had no ring on, Harper assumed the woman's parents had a wicked sense of humor. Even funnier was the fact that the woman's hair was stick straight.

Harper took the outstretched hand. "Harper Jennings—and I'm not a local."

Shirley snorted. "Yeah, I noticed. There are only about twelve hundred of us who live here year-round, so we kind of know who each other are."

"I'd imagine. I'm sorry this is happening to your town."

"Aren't we all?" She shook her head, her smile disappearing. "Locals have started calling this guy The Watcher, you know."

"Fitting name." Harper pushed away a shiver as her salad was placed in front of her. Between bites she asked, "You ever meet the other two women?"

Harper could sense the woman's need to talk, and she wanted to hear what she had to say. She had limited information before she came, stuff she'd found in a small local newspaper. Everyone wanted to talk about it, yet no one seemed anxious to share details about this case.

No one but Shirley.

"Oh, no. But I heard plenty about the other two victims. They were all the talk among locals. Everyone is freaking out about these murders."

"If you don't mind me asking, what do you know about the other victims? The whole situation has me horribly curious. It's like not being able to look away from an accident or something." Harper hoped she sounded casual enough. She just didn't want to draw any unnecessary attention to herself and her true motives for being here—not unless she had to.

"Oh, I get that. It's pretty much the same story, though. Both women were here alone. One, I think, had just gotten divorced and had come here to heal. The other came a few days ahead of her family for a vacation. When they got here . . ." Shirley's voice trailed off, and she shook her head. "You can fill in the blanks."

"Yes, I can." It sounded horrific.

Shirley's meal came, and she stuck one of the fries in her mouth. "You seem awfully curious. You weren't a friend or something, were you?"

Harper shrugged. "No, I wasn't. But I am a . . . reporter." Harper almost hated to share the information, especially since she wasn't here for a headline. She was here to help.

"Really? What kind?"

"Politics, mostly."

"Sounds exciting."

"It's not." It wasn't really what Harper wanted to do. She wanted her life to make a difference. She'd thought the career would be a good place to start. But, in the end, she'd realized just how much she hated the world of legislation. Everything about it left her feeling empty inside.

She really wanted to reevaluate her career sometime, but, at the same time, she needed a paycheck.

Shirley dipped her fry and raised it with a glob of ketchup on the end. "Well, if you really want answers, go visit Tom Brock down the street."

Harper took another bite of her salad, though her full attention was on Shirley. "Who's Tom Brock?"

"He's the town historian. He knows everything that goes on around this place, and he's done research on these murders. You know the cops aren't talking about anything. Everyone's so desperate to keep this hush-hush."

"Why?"

"It's not good for publicity. Without tourism, our economy around here would be nonexistent."

Harper could understand that. "Where can I find this Tom Brock?"

Shirley raised her burger, waiting to take a bite. "Easy to find. Go around the corner, and you'll see an old storefront that says Wetzel's Pretzels. Don't let that fool you. Tom lives in the apartment over the old shop."

"And you don't think he would find it odd if I just stopped by?"

"Oh, no. Not at all. He loves stuff like this. He'll talk your ear off. He's a widower, and I think he enjoys company."

Harper took another bite of her salad and nodded. Maybe she would do that.

The bell across the diner jangled, indicating the door had opened again. Harper looked over to see Sheriff Luke Wilder step inside.

He took his hat off—just barely—and nodded at anyone who turned to look. Then he took a seat at the bar, on the opposite end, and began bantering with the server on the other side. He didn't appear to see her.

Shirley followed her gaze. "And that is our new sheriff. Isn't he handsome? I mean, seriously, he looks like he could have stepped off the pages of *Field and Stream* magazine."

The man did have broad shoulders, a sculpted jaw, and thick hair. But it was more important to Harper that he was a man of character. She didn't know enough about him to form an opinion yet.

Had he looked into Billy? Did he believe her?

"How long has he been here in Fog Lake?"

"Maybe a year or something?" Shirley said. "He used to be a detective down in Atlanta. But after his dad died of cancer, he came back and took over as sheriff."

"Took over? Isn't there a process for that?" It sounded like nepotism at its best.

"Oh, sure there is. But everyone loved Daniel—he was Luke's dad. There was no doubt that Luke was going to get that job if he wanted it."

"Interesting." Harper finished her salad and dropped some money on the bar. She needed to check out this Tom guy before it got too late. "Thanks for talking."

"It was my pleasure. I'm here every night, doing what I do best. Running my mouth." Shirley chuckled at her own joke.

That was good to know, actually.

Just as Harper reached the door, Luke started that way also, pulling his coat back on and apparently abandoning his chance to eat.

The two nearly collided with each other, and, as their arms brushed, Harper felt a jolt of—something.

Shock?

Static electricity?

Whatever it was, Harper couldn't get away from the man fast enough.

Chapter Six

LUKE'S EYES narrowed when he saw Harper Jennings there.

He pressed his lips together and pushed open the door before stiffly saying, "Ladies first."

She stepped out. At least the woman had dressed for the area this time. Gone were her city shoes and clothing.

But after everything Luke had learned about her, he didn't like her being here. Not one bit. Even Harper's mother didn't trust her.

As he followed her out, the sound of the concert rang through the air, followed by cheering.

Luke was glad people were having fun. He just needed for them to be safe.

As the door closed behind them, Luke glanced down at Harper. He considered his words, quickly chewing on his options, before deciding he should call her out.

"I know who you are," he said.

Harper stopped there on the sidewalk and pivoted toward him. "I told you who I was."

"A reporter?"

Her expression darkened. "That's not why I'm here. I told you why I came."

"And I talked to your mom," Luke announced, watching her expression carefully.

Harper's face paled as her muscles seemed to loosen with shock for a moment. "At least you're doing your research."

Luke wasn't done yet. "She told me that you had a vendetta against your brother."

Harper's eyes narrowed, and she scoffed. "Well, that's her viewpoint, I suppose."

"She confirmed that he died and said your scar is from a car accident you were in."

Harper raised her chin. "She has no idea."

"Why would a mother lie about that?"

"There are plenty of reasons." Her voice sounded dull. "I could tell you all of them, but I'm certain you still wouldn't believe me. So I'll save my breath."

"So be it."

"I'll find Billy myself."

Luke startled. "That's not a good idea."

"If you're not going to listen to me then I have no other choice."

"Ms. Jennings—Harper—you might get yourself killed. I strongly advise against getting involved."

She said nothing.

Luke would stand here and argue with her, but he needed to pick up his sister.

Harper remained silent, just turned and walked away.

Luke watched her go.

That woman was something else. She was persuasive. Very persuasive.

But the best liars were.

His phone buzzed again. He listened as Deputy Dewey gave Luke an update on his sister, Ansley. She was currently sitting in the back of Dewey's squad car, and his deputy was waiting for Luke to arrive so he could figure out how to proceed.

It was just as well that Luke got away from here.

Because something about Harper Jennings got under his skin in a way few people could.

And he already had enough to worry about without adding her to his list of problems.

Harper tried to put her encounter with the sheriff out of her mind as she hurried down the street. If there was one thing she couldn't stand, it was cockiness, and the sheriff encompassed the word.

Of course, her mother hadn't helped Harper's case any. It shouldn't be a surprise that, after all these years, her mom was still angry. But that was okay. Harper had done the right thing when she'd left home. Though she mourned the fractured relationship, some things couldn't be undone.

Harper hadn't spoken with her mom in seven years, not since she'd been kicked out of the house. Even when Billy had died, Harper had decided not to attend the funeral. Not after the attack.

Sure, she hadn't seen his face. But she knew. In her gut, she'd known it was Billy in her apartment. He'd found her again and attempted to finish what he'd threatened as a teenager.

Harper drew her thoughts away from those dark times and glanced at the time on her phone. It was only eight o'clock.

Most businesses were still open at this hour. The darkness made it feel later.

As she turned the corner, the scenic harbor area came into view. The area was lit with atmospheric string lights and a nice dock where people could observe the beauty of the lake. On one side of the water, boats were harbored in neat slips. On the other side, a sectioned-off area in the water served as a beach during warm summer months.

Harper paused, sucked in a deep breath, and looked at the building beside her.

Here she was.

At Tom's place.

Harper stood by the door and swallowed hard. Maybe it was too late for an unexpected visit from a stranger. Despite that, she pounded on the door there anyway.

There was no answer.

Maybe this had been a bad idea. She'd come back tomorrow when she had a better sense of the town. When it wasn't so dark outside.

As she turned to walk away, she heard movement on the stairs.

Was someone coming down to answer?

Harper paused and waited.

She'd never been good at waiting. And right now, everything seemed even more urgent.

The first murder had happened four months ago. The second one six weeks ago. And now this one.

The killer seemed to be getting braver.

Time was of the essence when it came to figuring out who it was.

She no longer heard any movement.

However, there was a phone number scribbled on some paper by the door.

Trying to reach Tom? Call him. He may have taken his hearing aids out, and going down the steps takes him ten minutes because of his arthritis. Ha!

Harper raised her eyebrows. Okay, that seemed simple enough. The paper looked like it stayed there permanently, and she guessed that Tom had written the note himself.

She dialed the number, and a man with a scratchy voice answered on the second ring.

"My name is Harper Jennings. I'm a reporter, and I have a few questions about the town that I was hoping you could answer."

"Of course. Shirley told me you might be coming."

"Shirley? I just talked to her." Yet hearing his words brought her a strange comfort. She'd felt like she was intruding only seconds earlier. Now, she felt expected.

"She called just a few minutes ago."

Harper supposed that explanation made sense.

"Listen, my knees aren't what they used to be, so I'd rather not come downstairs. The outside door is unlocked. Why don't you come on up?"

She stared at the weathered gray door with the brass 628 on the front. She was certain that, when she opened this door, there would be a stairway leading to another door above. She'd seen apartments like these before.

"Sounds good. I'll see you in a moment."

With a touch of hesitation, Harper twisted the knob. The hinges creaked as the door opened.

She craned her neck upward, staring at the dark stairway leading up to another door, just as she'd suspected.

Her throat felt surprisingly dry as she reached for the light switch. She flipped it to the On position, but nothing happened.

Of course.

Harper's hesitation grew, but, despite that, she stepped inside.

The first step groaned under her weight and sent shivers scrambling over her skin.

Old buildings. They did that.

She took four more steps, her hand gripping the railing beside her like a lifeline. Suddenly, the door slammed shut behind her.

The hair on Harper's neck rose as pitch blackness enveloped her. Her heart thumped out of control at the uncertainty of not being able to see.

The wind, she realized. The wind had probably blown the door shut.

Harper didn't like the tight feeling in her gut.

She had to make a choice—and now.

Either rush upstairs to talk to Tom or rush back downstairs and flee.

Harper normally considered herself brave. But, right now, her instincts screamed to run. Something felt all wrong about this situation.

Her limbs quivered, and she hurried down the steps.

Just as she should have reached the door, something covered her mouth, silencing her. Something else—an arm—pinned her limbs together, capturing her.

Harper dropped her phone as a bag encased her head and strong arms lifted her off her feet.

Chapter Seven

"ANSLEY, WHAT WERE YOU THINKING?" Luke stared at his sister as she sat in the leather recliner that had been his father's favorite chair here in the family home.

His sister buried her hands in her face, her bleached-blonde hair falling over her eyes. "I don't know."

Her hunched position wasn't so much an indicator of sorrow. No, she was hungover and her adrenaline had worn off, leaving her angry and frustrated.

"You need to stay away from Zack Stephens, do you understand me?"

She raised her head, her lips pressed together, and a firestorm in her gaze. "You're not my dad!"

Luke had heard this argument before. "I'm not. But I told Dad I would watch out for you. And now you're going out drinking? Hanging out with Zack Stephens? Did he put you up to this?"

She shook her head, her furious rebellion returning. "No, we decided to do it together. We thought it would be fun."

"So the two of you were just sitting around, having a drink outside his place when you decided you should walk across the train trestle at night? When you decided you should spray paint a message on the stonework beneath it?"

"Yes, that's what happened."

Luke shook his head. "I don't believe it."

Red-rimmed eyes cast a scowl his way. "Well, believe it. I am capable of thinking for myself and making my own bad decisions."

"Oh, I completely agree that you're capable of making bad choices."

As soon as the words left Luke's mouth, he regretted them. He hung his head and squeezed his temples. When was he ever going to get this right? It felt like never. Having these conversations with his sister was something he hadn't wished upon himself.

No, life in Atlanta had been so much easier.

But how could he tell his dad no? His family needed him. And he felt like he was failing them over and over again.

Lord, give me the words, the wisdom.

Softening his voice, he knelt beside his sister. "Look, Ansley, I'm sorry if I spoke too harshly. I just don't want to see anything bad happen to you. I can't bear the thought of losing anyone else. Can you understand that?"

She wiped the tears under her eyes using a crumpled tissue. "I just want to feel alive again."

"There are other ways. Better ways."

"I can't think of any."

Luke bit his tongue. "Ansley . . ."

She shot to her feet. "Look, I just need some time alone. And I don't want another dad. I already had one, and he was great. I don't need a replacement. And I especially don't want it to be you. You didn't even want to come back here."

"Ansley, that's not true—"

But before he could finish, Ansley stormed up the stairs and slammed her door.

Luke stood, suddenly feeling an unbearable pressure bearing down on him. There was nothing he could say. Nothing at all. He didn't want to be Ansley's dad. He only wanted her to be safe. Couldn't she understand that?

He stepped outside onto the deck of his house. In the distance, he saw Fog Lake. His property stretched all the way to the shore.

A few months ago, he'd begun building a pergola there that he wanted to dedicate to his father. But the project sat unfinished. He blamed it on not having time. But, in truth, maybe he just didn't have the heart to complete it.

Chilly air cooled Luke's face, and crisp autumn leaves crunched beneath his feet. He leaned against the railing a moment before hanging his head.

Moving back here had been just as hard as he'd

thought it would be. He'd given up his job. His girlfriend had decided that breaking up with him was better than moving to Hickville—her words.

But it wasn't just that.

He'd traded not only his life but his essence to come here. No longer was he the guy who liked to hike and play baseball and who even sang in his church choir. No, he was a shadow of the person he used to be. Grief, responsibility, and a harsh lesson in selflessness had overwhelmed him.

And the most ironic part was that the very people he'd given up everything for seemed to hate him the most. Ansley. Jaxon. Even this town.

He'd never live up to his father.

His phone buzzed. It was the deputy who'd brought Ansley in—Abe Dewey. The man was in his mid-twenties and was the more reliable of his two deputies, but still lacked experience, tact, and personality. Luke had heard several college-aged tourists remarking that Dewey looked like James Dean with his wavy, light brown hair and aloof demeanor.

Luke didn't feel up to taking any more calls today. No, he needed competent deputies behind him. But Cruise and Dewey seemed more comfortable being meter readers than actual cops.

He wasn't sure why his father had hired them. Ms. Mary had once told Luke that his father witnessed Dewey rescue a bystander who stepped out in front of a car. He had hired Dewey on the spot, figuring someone that courageous would make a good deputy.

Luke pushed away the weariness from his voice as he answered the call.

"Luke, we just got a call from someone who said he heard screaming from inside the old Wetzel's Pretzels shop."

Adrenaline spiked his blood. "Can you check it out?"

"I'm here at Hanky's. There was a bar fight, and I'm taking statements. Cruise is managing the concert."

"I'll be right there."

The man dragged Harper up the stairs.

She sucked in a deep breath as fear coursed through her blood.

Scream, Harper. Scream.

Yet she couldn't.

Her vocal chords were frozen.

As were the man's.

He was silent. Wordless. Only releasing a grunt or two as his fingers dug into her skin.

After he stopped at the top of the stairs, Harper heard a creak—like a door opening. The next instant, her body slammed into a wall.

She gasped, her back aching at the jolt. She grabbed her shoulder and tried to make herself small, to draw back.

What would he do next?

Was this Billy? The Watcher? Would he finish what he'd started three years ago by running his knife across her throat, silencing her . . . forever?

Harper held back a cry.

The man still didn't speak.

All Harper could hear was herself breathing.

Do something, Harper. Don't just cower here.

The next instant, the bag was yanked from her head.

She blinked. Pitch blackness still surrounded her.

Where was the man? Was he still here? Was it Billy?

She jerked her head from left to right.

Harper saw nothing.

Was the man somehow watching her through the darkness?

Terror crawled over her skin at the thought.

Harper waited a few minutes. Tried to anticipate his next move. To guess what might happen.

Nothing.

Harper couldn't just stand still. She had to get away.

She rushed forward until she hit . . . a door? Yes, this had to be a door.

Harper found a knob. Twisted it.

It was no use.

The door was locked.

And no matter how her fingers moved and searched and scrambled, she couldn't get it undone.

Instead, she pounded on the door, screaming.

She'd found her voice again.

Thank goodness.

She screamed louder.

Surely someone had to hear her. Unless the concert drowned out the noise . . .

But Harper couldn't think like that.

How could she have been so stupid? That hadn't been Tom she'd talked to, had it? It had been the killer.

A new shiver of fright rushed through her.

Harper would have to think through those details later. Right now, she had to get out of here before the man—Billy?—killed her, just like he'd killed those three other women.

She stopped pounding for a moment and turned to look around. It was no use. There was only darkness here.

Cold, silent darkness.

And with every moment that passed, the chill inside her spread bigger, colder, fiercer.

"Why'd you come?" someone rasped.

Harper jumped so fast and hard that her elbow hit the wall behind her and another ache spread.

The man.

He was still here.

Still taunting her.

Did she recognize his voice? Was it Billy? Harper wanted to say yes. She wanted to be confident.

But she wasn't. She wasn't sure at all.

"Who are you?" She tried to sound stronger than

she was. It was no use. She was a quivering mess. Was this man going to kill her?

"I think you know that answer." The man's voice came out as a harsh, thick whisper.

Harper's eyes adjusted ever so slightly to the darkness, and a knife came into view. A knife and the gleam of the man's eyes.

He must be wearing all black from head to toe. And he stood in front of her.

He held the blade toward her. If Harper were to step forward, even an inch, it might stab her.

Her lungs seized as she realized just how close to death she was.

Then he was gone. A noise sounded in the distance. And silence.

Had he left?

Silence slithered around her. It was like a fog within itself. Thick. Squeezing. Enveloping.

Harper couldn't just stand here frozen.

She pounded on the wood again. Certainly someone outside could hear her. Except the concert drowned out everything with its loud drums and bass.

Harper bit back a cry.

No one would hear her over that music.

And she'd dropped her phone when the man grabbed her.

Panic wanted to claim her, but she wouldn't let it. She couldn't let it. Her survival right now depended on keeping a cool head.

No, that wasn't true. She wouldn't die up here. Eventually, she'd be able to find a way out.

Harper just had no idea where she was. What the place looked like.

All she knew was that it smelled bad in here. Really bad.

She coughed as she breathed in more of the odor.

What was that scent?

It almost smelled like old trash. Rotting food. Dirty socks.

But there was more.

Was that . . . death?

No, it couldn't be. Harper's imagination was going crazy.

Despite herself, she took a step back. Sucked in a few breaths to calm her racing heart. Then tried to think this through.

She just needed to yell and scream more. Get someone to notice she was up here. When the man had grabbed her, she'd screamed. Maybe someone had heard.

She turned around again, trying to get a better idea of her surroundings. But the darkness was too overwhelming.

Finally, a noise downstairs caught her ear.

Someone was here.

Help?

Or had the man returned?

Harper had no idea.

CHRISTY BARRITT

But she decided to take her chances and began pounding on the door again.

"Somebody, help me! Please! I'm up here!" Harper yelled until her voice was hoarse and she couldn't scream anymore.

She heard more sounds. More footsteps. Heard the door rattling.

Help.

Help was here.

Relief burst through her with so much force that tears nearly popped out of her eyes.

"Stand back!" a voice ordered.

She did as she was told, hardly able to contain herself as she waited. She wanted out of this place. Now.

Something hit the door. Hit the door again.

Wood splintered. Splintered more.

Finally, light cut through the darkness.

And Sheriff Luke Wilder stepped inside, looking larger than life with the street light behind him illuminating his broad figure.

He shone his flashlight toward her, and when the beam hit her face, he rushed forward. "Harper?"

She reached forward, desperate for something—or someone—to ground her. Her fingers hit his fabric jacket and immediately her heart slowed. She was alive and everything would be okay.

"Are you all right?" Strains of soft sincerity mellowed Luke's voice.

"I . . . I think so."

64

Two deputies came in behind him, also with flashlights. The bright beams helped to cut through some of the darkness, but this place was just still so black and unnerving.

"What happened?" Luke asked, still kneeling in front of her.

She shivered as she remembered. "Someone . . . grabbed me. Put me up here. Threatened me with a knife."

Luke leaned closer, gaze locked on hers. "The person who put you here . . . is he gone?"

Harper nodded. "He . . . left. I think. It was so dark. I could hardly see."

"I want to hear more in a moment. I need you to stay put for a second while we check out the rest of the place and make sure it's secure. Okay?"

"Of course."

"Sheriff, there's something you're going to want to see in here," one of the deputies called.

Something internal tugged at Harper. She knew she should stay against the wall where the sheriff had left her. But something unseen seemed to compel her —something she wasn't able to stop. She followed Luke, desperate to know what else had been found.

With the flashlights spreading light in the room, more details came into focus. Harper realized she had indeed been in an apartment, but it looked old and abandoned.

She stepped down the hallway, staying close to the sheriff. Not wanting to be alone again.

He stopped at a bedroom door.

The beam of his light hit a body.

On the bed.

And suddenly Harper knew exactly what the scent was she'd been smelling.

Chapter Eight

LUKE HEARD the gasp behind him.

He turned, his back muscles tightening. Harper stood there. Her face looked paler than just a few minutes earlier. Her eyes wider. Her trembles deeper.

He should have known the woman would follow him. He started to scold her, but seeing this dead body was reprisal enough.

He broadened his stance, trying to shield her from the scene. Or was he shielding the scene from Harper? The jury was out on that now.

But Luke knew one thing for sure: Harper, with all of her theories and her twisted past, was terrified. Whatever had happened here tonight had shaken her to the core. He feared the woman might pass out.

"Dewey, take Ms. Jennings out to the squad car," Luke ordered. "She doesn't need to be in here. And don't take your eyes off her until I get down there."

"Yes, sir," his deputy said.

Harper started to say something, but Luke stopped her. "You can't be in here. I need to talk to you, but first, I've got to process this scene. Do you understand?"

She nodded, looking too dazed and in shock to argue. "Okay."

Dewey led her outside.

As soon as she was gone, Luke turned to Cruise, who looked worse off than Harper had. In fact, he looked like he might throw up again.

Luke bit back a sigh. "Cruise, see if you can get some lights on in this place. Then put up some crime-scene tape. No one gets through, understand?"

"Yes, sir."

With all the confusion cleared from around him, Luke took another step into the bedroom. As far as he knew, no one had lived in this old apartment in years. So how had Harper ended up here? And whose body was in the bedroom?

Luke shone his light on the man lying sprawled on the twin-sized bed. As the beam hit the victim's face, Luke sucked in a breath.

Tom Brock. The town's historian. A man who never bothered anyone.

And he was dead.

Freshly dead, it appeared, based on *rigor mortis*.

Luke leaned down to examine the man closer. There was no visible sign of blood. No signs of struggle.

So what had happened to the elderly man? Had

he died of natural causes? Or had the town's killer done this also? And why here?

The mode of death didn't match the perp's pattern. He'd only killed brunettes before this. Young women. Pretty. Single.

Tom was none of those things.

But it seemed like too much of a coincidence to believe they had a second killer in town.

Luke had a lot of questions for Harper. Why was she in the apartment? Did she have anything to do with this man's death?

He would say no. The woman had looked truly terrified. But he couldn't take anything for granted or jump to conclusions.

He needed to get his medical examiner here. Now.

Harper felt like she'd been sitting in the back of the squad car for hours.

She didn't even have her phone, so she couldn't check the time. The deputy—Deputy Dewey—had brought her a blanket and some coffee, so she shouldn't complain.

But the trembles rushing through her felt just short of overwhelming. And the shakes wouldn't stop, no matter how hard she willed them to do just that.

Today had clawed at her core, leaving deep gashes in any peace of mind she'd tried to hold onto.

Every time Harper closed her eyes, the attack began replaying in her mind. The feel of the bag over her head. The man's harsh whisper. The darkness.

She trembled again.

So much for acting like the strong, professional woman she was. Right now she felt like a whimpering fool who might turn into a puddle at any minute.

"That must have been scary," Deputy Dewey said, glancing back from the front of the patrol car. "I'm sorry it happened to you."

Harper observed him a moment. He had dark, short hair. An average build. A quiet demeanor.

He'd seemed more competent than the other deputy—she thought his name was Cruise. But both were on the younger side and seemed to keep one eye on Sheriff Wilder all the time. Were they inexperienced and therefore unsure or did they fear displeasing the man?

"It was scary," Harper finally said. "Then again, I guess that's the way this whole town has been feeling lately with a killer on the prowl."

"You can say that again. I've never seen anything like this."

"You grow up here?" she asked, mostly trying to distract herself.

"Mostly. Then again, most people around here say that. They think they want to leave the small town that's trapping them, only to come back later when they realize what a treasure it is." He glanced at her again. "You from a small town?"

"Raleigh, North Carolina. Not exactly small."

"Nah, that's considered big city to most people around here."

She glanced at the charming town around her. "It's a shame this place is tainted now."

Dewey glanced around also. "Yeah, it really is. But she'll recover. She always does."

Harper shifted, already tired of small talk and feeling antsy, as if she might lose her mind if she stayed in this vehicle any more. "How much longer?"

"The sheriff is still assessing the crime scene, but I think the ME is almost finished."

As if Luke had heard her, he appeared from the doorway. He knocked on the window, and Deputy Dewey climbed out. The two whispered a few things to each other, and then Luke opened her door.

"I need to take you to the station," he started. "It will be a little more comfortable in my office than the car."

The sheriff cupped her elbow and led her to his SUV. He helped her inside, closed the door, and then climbed behind the wheel. The vehicle roared to life.

He turned on the heat, and warmth flooded inside. Despite that, Harper still pulled the blanket closer. She'd taken it with her—and her coffee.

"I'm surprised you can leave this scene," she finally said.

"Deputy Cruise will stand guard. The scene will be roped off, and no one else will be able to enter until the apartment is cleared."

"I see."

Luke took off toward the sheriff's office and, a few minutes later pulled into a space out front. He ushered her into his office.

The sheriff didn't seem quite as gruff as he had during their earlier encounter. Compassion had ebbed into his gaze. But Harper had no doubt he could turn off his kindness in an instant if he wanted.

Harper sat in the chair across from him—the same stiff one she'd sat in earlier. But this time, instead of taking his place behind the desk, Luke sat beside her. He leaned on his knees, a pad of paper in hand.

"You want to tell me what happened tonight?" he started.

A lump formed in her throat. Harper didn't want to relive the ordeal. Nor did she want to let him know that she'd naively gone to see Tom, thinking he might have answers. She should have waited until morning. Or taken someone with her.

But she had no one to take along. And, even if she had waited until morning, the results might have been the same. Nothing made sense right now.

"I met a woman at the diner." Harper rubbed her throat to ward away the ache there. "She was very chatty and told me I should talk to the town historian if I really wanted some details on the murders."

"About the murders?" His voice held an edge of surprise.

"Yes, about the murders."

"What was this woman's name?"

"Shirley Cue."

Luke stared at her. "Shirley Cue?"

"Yes, Shirley Cue. She's a local. You should know her. She said she goes to the diner every night. You could ask the others there tonight about her."

He gave her another look that showed her that not all was right with her statement.

Harper lowered her head. "Please don't tell me there's no one here with that name."

"Shirley Cue?" Luke repeated.

Her head pounded harder. Of *course* that woman had been a part of this. Otherwise, Harper would have never known where to go. "I knew the name was cutesy and weird, but some people name their kids weird things. I don't even question it anymore. But you're saying that woman . . . you don't know her?"

She needed to hear it with her own ears, to make sure she wasn't making ill-informed assumptions again.

"I don't know her," Luke said quietly, using a surprising amount of courtesy when he could have easily scoffed.

Her head dipped even lower as her cheeks heated. "I can't believe I was that stupid."

"Don't beat yourself up. Now, I need to hear what else happened."

Harper told him a recap of the evening's events, and Luke listened, taking a few notes on his pad of paper.

"And that's it," Harper finished, rubbing her hands against her jeans. "You found me, and you also found . . . a dead body."

She shivered as she remembered all of it.

Luke nodded slowly, and she knew she was missing something. She just didn't know what, nor did she want to feel like more of a fool. But she had to know.

"Look, I know I screwed up," Harper said. "What are you thinking? Just tell me. I can handle the truth."

He shrugged, glanced at his notepad, and then pulled his gaze up to hers. "Tom didn't live in that building, Harper."

"But—"

"It's been abandoned for years."

That couldn't be right. There was some kind of miscommunication going on here. "There was a note outside with Tom's phone number."

"We didn't find a note. In fact, the numbers on the door weren't there until sometime today. They're new."

All the color and life drained from Harper as a new realization hit her.

"What is it, Harper?"

"Six twenty eight." She ran a hand over her face as the truth clicked in her mind. "That's Billy's birthday. How could I not have seen this earlier?"

Luke glanced beside him in his Explorer as he drove Harper back to her motel. She suddenly didn't seem like such a career-focused woman anymore. No, Harper almost reminded him of a lost, scared little girl.

Maybe his first impression of the woman had been wrong. Maybe he'd even been too hard on her.

"Do you think Billy did this?" Luke's voice cut into the silence of the ride. He still thought the idea was outlandish, but he wanted to know how her thoughts were evolving. After all, someone—two people, for that matter—had targeted Harper this evening. There had to be a reason for it.

Harper stared out the window. "I don't know. I want to say yes. But . . . I just don't know. The numbers on the door . . ."

"It could be a coincidence."

"Maybe. But I doubt it."

Luke doubted it also, but he didn't want to tell Harper that. "You didn't recognize the man's voice?"

"No, he was whispering. I wish . . . I wish I knew more. But maybe my gut instincts aren't what I thought they were."

He glanced over at her again. Harper fit the profile of the other victims. She was practically setting herself up on an altar as a sacrifice for this guy. Yet the man had the chance to kill Harper tonight and hadn't. Luke was going to have to turn that over in his head some more.

But one fact remained. "I don't think you should stay in town, Harper."

She jerked her gaze toward him, as if his words had startled her. "How can I leave?"

"Easy. Just go back to DC. Return to your life. Leave us to figure this out."

"But I can help! I know Billy." Harper's voice rose with passion, conviction, and determination.

Luke made sure to soften his voice before he asked, "What if this isn't Billy? What if he really is dead?"

Harper opened her mouth as if to offer a quick retort but closed it again. She pressed her lips together then finally said, "Why did this person target me, then? Why else would someone target me?"

"I don't have that answer yet."

He pulled to a stop in front of the Whistling Pines Motel. Before she could object, he hopped out. Luke would walk her up to her room and check it out before leaving. And nothing Harper said was going to change his mind. If she wasn't leaving town, then he would at least ensure she was safe.

"You don't have to do this," she said, climbing from the SUV and falling into step beside him.

"I want to."

"Okay then." Harper wrapped her arms across her chest as they climbed the steps toward the third floor.

Luke kept a hand on her back, sensing she needed someone to steady her right now. As the wind swept over her, the faint scent of honeysuckle drifted his way. It seemed like such an unassuming scent for such a complex woman.

As they reached her room, she pulled out her key. But her hand trembled so badly that the metal clanged against the knob, not making it into the lock itself.

Luke took it from her, unlocked her room, and opened the door. "Let me check things out first."

"You think—"

"I don't think anything. I'm just being cautious."

She nodded and stood against the wall as Luke checked the bathroom, the shower, and under the beds. It was all clear.

"Lock your door tonight," he warned anyway. No more dead bodies. No more victims. There had already been too many.

"Don't worry. I will. Are you going back to the crime scene?"

Luke nodded, realizing he had a long night ahead of him. He suddenly felt like his workload from Atlanta had been transported to Fog Lake. "Yeah, I am."

Harper looked up at him with wide eyes. Her expression didn't strike Luke as the expression of someone hungry to advance her career. No, at the moment, she looked like someone who'd been caught in the crosshairs.

She cleared her throat. "You think the same

person killed Tom? I'm assuming he's the one you found dead."

Luke didn't confirm her theory. No, he had to inform the next of kin first. "I don't know yet if the same killer struck again. It's too early to say."

"This crime doesn't fit the rest."

"I know."

Harper nodded and stepped back, as if realizing the conversation was over. "Okay then. Thank you for everything."

"You're welcome." Luke reached into his pocket. "I found this. I think it belongs to you."

He held out her cell phone. "Thank you. I dropped it when—"

"I know." Luke paused before walking away. "And Harper? I really would consider going back to DC if I were you. Fog Lake may not be safe for you."

The look in her eyes told him she wouldn't be doing that. In fact, she looked more determined than ever to see this case through until the end.

Chapter Nine

HE STOOD at the edge of town, just out of sight. Blending in. Unseen.

Just like the fog intermingled with this place.

The Native Americans who'd once lived in this area thought the fog had special powers. The Pogorip said that the gods used the low-lying clouds to conceal their presence before battle, allowing them to win.

In return, the Pogorips had offered sacrifices to the gods through a process called bloodletting.

In order to get what they wanted, they expelled blood as a sacrifice.

This pleased their gods.

It was fascinating, really.

But he liked the idea.

He liked thinking that he was contributing also. He wasn't sure whom he was making his sacrifice to—he certainly didn't believe in the gods of nature. But expelling blood . . . being at one with nature . . . it made him feel a connection deep down in his soul.

He *could* wait again before feeding his hunger. Before pleasing unseen gods with life blood that evaporated like the clouds in demanding sunlight.

He'd waited six weeks last time before his sacrifice.

Killing wasn't always about timing, though. Sometimes, it was about finding the right person.

And that person had waltzed into town.

She was here in Fog Lake.

And she was perfect. So perfect. Everything on his list.

Seeing her had made his hunger grow with an insatiable vengeance.

He fisted his hands, wishing he had his knife. But he didn't. No, there were too many people around listening to that stupid concert. The music grated on his nerves.

He hated almost everything about this town. But he was looking forward to the Fog and Hog festival. It would be the perfect timing for another kill.

Which was one reason he didn't kill the woman tonight. That hadn't been his plan.

And nothing changed his plans.

Not even Tom Brock. Tom was never supposed to see him with that flute.

He became a liability.

That liability had been eliminated.

Tom's death hadn't brought the same satisfaction.

But luring the woman to the scene had.

Feeling her fear had been invigorating.

But it wasn't her time to go.

Not yet.

However, he couldn't wait six weeks this time. He could feel the growls from deep inside him. Growls that needed to be satisfied. Hunger pains.

He stepped back into the shadows and watched. Watched the sheriff escort her to the motel room. Room 309. He'd seen her there earlier.

But a motel room wouldn't work. It was too risky.

He'd have to think of something else—another way to complete his hunt.

At once, he fisted his hands together. Regret began to claw at him, almost as if it were personified. As if the emotion were a person living inside him, fighting to get to the surface and take control.

His father had taught him all about it.

Except, his father had called it hunting. Had shown him how to wait for just the right moment. How to get his prey in his crosshairs.

And then how to steal life and breath from a being that had once been thriving.

His smile returned.

He couldn't wait to see the terror on her face when he finally revealed himself. When she realized he'd been hiding in plain sight. When she understood finally just how clueless she'd been.

His smile curled higher at the edges of his lips.

The upcoming reunion was going to be wonderful. Simply wonderful.

And no one could stop it. Especially not Sheriff Luke Wilder.

Chapter Ten

HARPER SAT up in bed and raked a hand through her hair. Her head pounded from her sleepless night. As soon as she'd closed her eyes, she'd been transported back in time.

She'd been nineteen, lying in her bed, trying to sleep.

But she'd woken with a start.

Billy—her foster brother—was standing beside her bed, staring at her. He'd been sixteen at the time.

"Billy, are you sleepwalking?" Harper sat up, her heart still racing.

Billy said nothing, only stared at her.

But he didn't look confused. No, he looked lucid. And what was that other emotion? Was it satisfaction?

That thought chilled her.

"Billy? What are you doing? Go back to bed." Harper finally found her voice, but the words sounded fragile as they left her lips.

He kept staring.

Harper's gaze traveled downward, and she sucked in a breath.

He held a knife.

And that look in his eye?

It wasn't satisfaction. It was worse. It was evil.

"I dream about blood," he whispered.

Harper's fingers clawed into her sheets. She should scream. Call for help. Do something.

Yet she felt frozen.

No, no, no! Do something, Harper.

But she couldn't.

"You need help, Billy," she finally whispered.

"No one can help me."

"Are you going to hurt me?"

"Not yet."

Back in the present, Harper pulled the sheets around her and pushed away the tears that had come to her eyes. She sucked in deep, hungry breaths, and her heart raced out of control.

She'd known coming here to Fog Lake would be challenging. She'd known it would be hard.

But knowing all of that hadn't changed how awful the actual reality of it was.

Maybe Sheriff Luke Wilder was right. Maybe she should go back to DC. Go to work. Write up articles after attending mind-numbing press conferences. Forget that any of this had ever come to her attention.

A long line of people would be there waiting to take her job. If she didn't need to support herself, she'd tell any one of them they could have her position. But life wasn't quite that easy, especially without a support system to fall back on.

Besides, Harper couldn't live with herself if someone else died—not while knowing she had the opportunity to stop these dastardly acts from happening.

Shoving the thoughts aside for a moment, Harper forced herself out of bed.

It was a new day, and she had to figure out her plan. Simply coming to town and hoping the answers would fall into her lap was foolish. Too foolish. When that happened, it would be another repeat of last night: an experience that seemed too good to be true —because it was.

No, Harper needed to be proactive here. The problem was, she wasn't sure where to start. The sheriff sure wasn't going to help her.

She quickly got ready and pulled on some jeans and a cable-knit sweater. She threw her hair back into a sloppy bun, knowing good and well that her curly tendrils would escape. Then she was out the door.

On the way to her car, she grabbed a honey bun from the vending machine, knowing she needed to eat something. She hadn't had one of these in years. Years.

Holding the edge of the wrapper between her teeth, she fished through her purse and found her keys. After climbing into her car, she programmed an address into her GPS. Twenty minutes later, she'd pulled around to the other side of the lake to the lane where Amy Mintel's cabin was located. Elk Row Lane.

Harper knew she wouldn't be able to get inside, but that was okay. She just wanted to get a feel for the area. For Amy. For the crime.

Early morning fog hung over the area, as it usually did. The gray clouds settled in the valleys and over the water and between the trees. As they shifted it was almost as if puffs of moisture were living things with a mind of their own, things that could decide what to conceal and what to reveal.

Just like her neighbor Ian had said.

Harper shivered, took a bite of her honey bun, and let the overwhelmingly gooey taste of sugar-covered carbs delight her taste buds. She made a mental note to head to the grocery store later, though. She couldn't keep eating like this.

She pulled to a stop at the end of the lane and surveyed the area in front of her. Four cabins stood on the lake. Each was small and had a log exterior. Several docks jutted out into the water like fingers clawing to the surface.

Harper climbed out, wiped the crumbs of her breakfast from her shirt, and walked toward the lake. Maybe she should be scared. Maybe she was stupid to come here alone.

But Billy only ever struck at night, and she felt certain he wouldn't harm her now.

She hoped those gut instincts were correct. But if

she was going to find answers, she would have to do it alone. Harper had no one to tag along with her. And that was okay. She was used to being alone. She'd had to learn to cope with her fear.

All the cabins appeared to be empty. Strange for this time of the year.

Then again, Harper could understand why no one had wanted to stay. She couldn't blame them after what had happened here.

She pulled her arms across her chest as she paused at the lake's shore and breathed in a deep gulp of fresh mountain air.

There was nothing like it.

She sure didn't get that same sense of clean air in DC. Instead, she got smog and car exhaust.

Maybe her heart had always been in the mountains.

She and Joe had liked to come to the mountains together. Not to Fog Lake, but to the national parks closer to DC, just over the border in Maryland and in West Virginia. They'd hiked the trails and enjoyed picnic lunches and had taken extraordinary pictures together.

A faint smile brushed Harper's lips. Those had been happy days. Really happy days.

She and Joe had dated for six months—six wonderful months.

Until he'd broken up with her.

He'd told her he dealt with craziness on his job every day, and he couldn't stand for it to bleed into his personal life as well. He needed a partner without drama.

He'd told her that after she'd been attacked, and her life had been turned upside down.

After Billy had broken into her apartment and sliced open her throat, leaving her only a half-inch from death.

There had been no evidence on how he'd gotten into her place. He left no evidence behind either. And the police had no suspects.

But Harper had known it was Billy.

The event had turned her upside down. It had changed her.

And Joe couldn't handle those changes.

It was probably just as well. After all, Harper had gotten a glimpse of what the rest of her life would look like if she stayed with this man. He was a cop, and she'd realized that work would always be his first priority. It would always be his driving force. And everything else—including her—would take second place.

Just like it had with her father.

And that was no way to live. It wasn't what Harper envisioned for her family or her future. Though it hurt when their relationship ended, it was for the best.

She didn't regret it. But she did feel alone sometimes. Most of the time, for that matter. The people in her life who were supposed to offer her unconditional love had put an awful lot of conditions on her presence in their lives. If her mom, dad, and boyfriend couldn't accept her for who she was, she had little hope that anyone ever would.

She liked to pretend that she was strong. That she could handle it. That she could face being alone for the rest of her life.

But sometimes she just wanted more.

She shoved aside those thoughts and made her way to the cabin. There was still crime-scene tape at the door, indicating this was the correct one.

Harper wouldn't break the law and try to enter the place. She just wanted a glimpse inside, maybe from a window. Being here probably wouldn't help her to prove anything, but at least it would give her a feel for what had happened.

And it definitely beat doing nothing.

After working all night, Luke stopped by his house that morning. For the last several hours he'd been investigating the scene in the apartment where Tom had been found and trying to put together the pieces. He'd stay home just long enough to clean himself up, grab a bite to eat, and then he had to get back to work.

The people in this town were depending on him to find answers.

Luke was depending on himself to find answers.

He'd just heard back from the ME. Tom Brock

had died from a fatal mix of his medications. The man had been on plenty—for his heart, his blood pressure, acid reflux, vitamin D.

Tom must have gotten his pills mixed up and taken too many. Some who knew him had been worried that he was suffering with the early stages of dementia.

Had Tom wandered into that old apartment building after taking his medicine? Had the mistake been fatal?

Luke didn't know for sure. But he had a hard time buying it.

Especially since Harper ended up at that exact location.

He put his belt with his holster and other gear onto the kitchen counter and felt the weight of everything that had happened pressing on him.

"Hey," someone said.

Boone.

His younger brother stepped out from the back bedroom with a cup of coffee in hand.

"Morning," Luke said, wondering how his brother could look so perky.

Oh, that was right. His brother had gotten to sleep last night. Sleep could do wonders for a person's mental state.

"You look terrible." Boone's eyebrows pushed together. "I heard there was another body and about Tom Brock. It's been the talk of the town."

"I'm sure it has been."

"Any closer to finding answers?" Boone handed him a cup of coffee.

Luke accepted the outstretched mug, took a long sip, and shook his head. "Nope, not really. Whoever is behind this . . . he's not leaving any evidence."

"Well, I saw a line of cars leaving town yesterday. It's not looking too good for business."

Luke leaned against the doorway to the kitchen, knowing he needed a mental break—however brief. Coffee and a quick talk with his brother might just do the trick. "I know. I'm doing everything I can. I assure you."

Boone sat at the breakfast bar, still facing Luke. He shoved the newspaper aside, his full attention on their conversation.

Luke's brother ran a camping store on the outskirts of town. He'd been an Army Ranger before moving back here to marry his high school sweetheart. But Katherine had a tragic accident while she and Boone were hiking on their honeymoon.

That had been five years ago, and Luke didn't think Boone had gotten over losing her. Locals still suspected Boone was secretly responsible for her death.

For that reason, Boone much preferred to interact with the town's visitors.

Their family had been through so much over the past several years. First losing Katherine in the hiking accident. Then losing their father to cancer. Their youngest brother, Jaxon, was serving in the Middle

East right now. When he was back in the States, he never came home. Ansley, the baby of the family, had taken their father's death the hardest and had dealt with it by rebelling, by trying to numb her pain with alcohol, men, and acts of utter stupidity.

And Luke somehow felt like the person who needed to hold everyone together.

It was a big job. A hard job. And most of the time, he felt ill-equipped to do it.

"What's on your schedule today?" Boone asked, still downing his coffee.

Luke felt exhausted just thinking about everything he needed to get done. "I'm going to revisit the crime scene. Check in with the crime lab. With the ME. We just need one clue that will break this case. Just one."

"And you don't have that yet, I assume."

Luke remembered the woman who'd come into the police station yesterday. Harper Jennings. He remembered her theory. Remembered how she'd been swept up into the crime from the moment she'd set foot in this town.

Then he remembered the conversation he'd had with Harper's mom. Her warnings to Luke about Harper.

At first, Luke had wanted to dismiss her. Part of him still wanted to.

But somehow Harper Jennings did seem connected with all of this. He'd be wise to keep an eye on her. Luke also needed to check out whether or not Billy Jennings had really died. He would put a call into the police in the area where the accident had supposedly happened. The task would be harder since Luke couldn't even find a record of the man's death. But Harper had given him the name of the city and the date of the accident.

"No, we don't have anything yet," Luke finally said.

"Some people were throwing out theories at the tackle shop yesterday."

Luke paused. He could only imagine what people were saying. "Like what?"

"Like the guy behind these murders is a ghost who's coming back for revenge."

Luke rolled his eyes. "I don't believe in ghosts."

"You have to admit it's strange. The way these women die . . . it's eerily similar to the massacre—"

"Ghosts don't exist, Boone." Luke cut his brother off and ran a hand over his face.

He had enough on his plate without listening to crazy theories. And in a town like Fog Lake, which seemed to be a magnet for hippies and other earthy types, there were plenty of crazy theories to go around.

"Okay, okay." Boone raised his hands in surrender. "Just thought it was interesting."

Luke glanced around the kitchen. "You seen Ansley yet?"

"She was asleep in her room last time I checked. I don't think she's working at the zipline today. Why?"

"Just wondering."

"I'll keep an eye on her. You just worry about this case."

Luke nodded, too tired to argue. Unfortunately, Ansley seemed to need a whole army to keep an eye on her lately.

He slipped upstairs to get ready, wondering what this new day had in store for him. Part of him didn't even want to find out.

Harper's phone rang, and she saw it was her sister Paige. Still standing on the misty shore near the cabin where Amy Mintel had died, she put her cell to her ear.

"Hey, Paige. What's going on?" Harper scanned the area around her again, looking for a sign of anything that might be out of place. Everything appeared serene and quiet.

So why was she so on edge? Then again, was there ever a time since her attack when she wasn't jumpy?

"I thought someone should check on you." Paige was twenty years old and one of the foster kids her parents had adopted. She'd been nine when Harper had first met her, and Harper had been sixteen.

Most of her adopted brothers and sisters wouldn't talk to Harper anymore, but Paige was different.

Paige and Harper had bonded, and Paige had been devastated when Harper left. She'd done her best to stay in touch with the girl. It had become easier now that Paige was out of the house and on her own.

"I'm doing fine." Harper pulled her arms tighter across her chest, suddenly realizing just how alone she was out here. After her attack last night, she really should be more careful.

Courage isn't the absence of fear, but the ability to face what scares you.

She glanced around again. The mountains stared back at her, but nothing and no one else.

A shiver ran down her spine. How could the fact that there was utter solitude out here be both comforting and disturbing? How could the isolation feel like both a friend and an enemy?

Harper chided herself for being paranoid. She'd checked behind her on the way here. No one had followed her. She was alone.

"Where are you?" Paige asked.

Harper turned back toward the expanse of water before her. "Fog Lake."

"Fog Lake? Where is Fog Lake, and why would you go there?" Paige's voice rose with an animated curiosity that Harper had always loved.

Probably because it reminded Harper of herself.

But her smile quickly faded as the truth slithered back into her mind. "Because there have been murders here, and they match Billy's MO."

Paige went dead silent for several seconds until saying, "Billy is dead . . ."

"What if he isn't?"

Paige went silent again. "He died in that accident. The police said so."

"His body was burned beyond recognition. What if he set the whole thing up? What if he wants everyone to believe he died?"

Paige let out a long breath. "I'm not sure what to think about that. But let's just say he is alive. You think . . . you think he's on a murder spree?"

"I could be wrong. I *hope* I'm wrong. But . . . everything matches, Paige. I just couldn't sit back and do nothing. I have to figure this out."

"I get that. But you have to think about yourself also. Why don't you just tell someone what you know and leave? You don't need to stay."

Harper scowled as she remembered doing just that. "I did tell someone—the sheriff—and he didn't take me seriously. In fact, he called Mom, who told him that I had a vendetta against Billy and shouldn't be taken seriously."

"That sounds like Mom."

Yes, it did. And, even after all these years, that realization still stung—the realization that her mother loved Billy more than she'd ever loved Harper. "She still hasn't forgiven me."

"Well, Billy always did cast that spell on her. And you held too much power—power to crack the perfect family image she wanted to create. She was afraid you were going to ruin things for her. She loved being held in high esteem in the community."

Harper swallowed hard. She thought she'd put those hurts from her childhood behind her, but maybe she never fully would. After all, if you didn't have the unconditional love of your family, where would you ever find it?

Harper pulled her sweater closer, realizing that it was chillier out here than she'd anticipated. Or had memories from her past swept back into her life like a frigid tornado that made everything ache with unbearable cold?

"Paige, when was the last time you saw Billy? Before he supposedly died, of course."

"Me? Oh, sheesh. Well . . . it was probably five years ago when he left home. Why?"

Five years ago . . . Billy would have been nineteen. "Does anyone in the family talk about him?"

"Not really. Although, I did run into Shari McKibben a year or so ago, and she mentioned something about seeing Billy a few weeks before he died."

Harper's back straightened. Shari McKibben? Shari had been a friend of their other sister, Cora. Billy had liked hanging out with them, and Shari had really liked Billy. At least, that's what Harper had heard.

"What did she say?" Harper asked.

"Hmm . . . I was only half listening because, honestly, I don't really care about Billy. But I think I recall Shari saying that Billy looked different."

"Different how?"

"I don't know. She almost made it sound like he'd

had plastic surgery."

"Plastic surgery?" Harper wanted to make sure she'd heard correctly.

Billy had always been a good-looking guy. He'd been kind of scrawny with a Roman nose and dark hair. He'd had startling blue eyes—eyes that Harper's mom had loved. All Billy had to do was look at her with those baby blues, and anything he wanted was his.

"Yeah, I'm not sure about the details. She just said she didn't recognize him until he said something to her. She said he looked like a totally different person. He'd even dyed his hair red."

Red? Red like her motel neighbor, Ian?

Another shiver snaked up her spine. That new tidbit of information made all of this a little more complex, didn't it? Harper could be staring at Billy and she wouldn't realize it.

"Listen, could you call Shari and find out more details? I need to know how he looked." The urgency to learn more pressed in on her, and Harper knew she wouldn't rest until she had more information.

"Harper, you do realize he's probably dead."

Harper's stomach clenched. "I know. I just . . . I just need to know."

As Harper ended the call, she heard a footstep behind her. She dropped her phone and twirled around, swallowing a scream.

What if Billy was alive—and what if he'd found her?

Chapter Eleven

"I DIDN'T MEAN to scare you." Luke raised his hands, a wave of guilt rushing through him.

He'd been certain Harper had heard him coming. He'd made no secret of it. But apparently, she'd been more wrapped up in her phone conversation than he'd given her credit for.

Her shoulders dropped, and her hand went to the skin on her throat. "I thought you . . ."

"Were a killer?"

She straightened her back, as if the moment of panic had passed, and shrugged. "Maybe."

Luke picked up her phone and handed it back. "Doesn't look like it was broken."

"Thank you." She shoved the device into her back pocket and drew in a long, deep breath.

Standing beside her, Luke looked out over the lake. He'd always loved this place. Loved the serenity it brought with it.

But now that serenity felt shattered. And it wasn't just Luke who felt it. No, the whole town knew they were on shaky ground.

"What are you doing here?" Luke asked.

"I just wanted to see where the murder took place. I didn't really think I would discover anything. I just wanted a feel for it."

"You're brave being out here alone."

"I don't know if I'd call it brave. Maybe desperate is a better word."

Luke nodded slowly, not trying to alarm Harper but feeling the desperate need to talk some sense into the woman. "That guy could have killed you last night."

A shiver seemed to capture her muscles, but she looked away from Luke, like she didn't want to acknowledge the possible truth in his words.

"I realize that," Harper said. "Believe me, I do."

"I just don't want to see someone else get hurt." Luke shifted. "You shouldn't be here, Harper."

"You keep saying that. Yet here I am. I promise, I'll try not to get in your way."

"This town can't handle another murder." His voice sounded low and full of warning, even to his own ears.

Her startled eyes met his. "I'm here because I don't want another murder either."

Before Luke could retort, his phone rang. It was Deputy Cruise.

"Sheriff, we just got a call," he started. "Someone

saw Benny Rasmussen out near Tom's place yesterday. The two of them had been arguing about some family history, apparently. Tom was going to publish a new book that made Benny's family look bad. What do you want me to do?"

"I'll go pay Benny a visit." Benny lived like a hermit in an old cabin up in the mountains, only coming down when he needed something like gas or water or to get his fix of trouble. All the locals knew to stay away from the man.

But that didn't mean everyone did stay away.

Though Luke didn't want to believe Benny may have killed Tom, he had to check it out.

Luke shoved his phone back into his pocket. "I've got to go. I'd feel better if you didn't stay here alone."

He expected Harper to argue, but she didn't. No, she nodded, almost defeated, and walked back to her car.

But when they got there, they paused.

One of her tires was flat.

***

Harper knelt beside her car. "How did this happen?"

Luke squatted next to her and examined the rubber. As his fingers slid along the side of the tire, he let out a little grunt. "Someone slashed it."

Harper's lungs froze at his words. "What?"

"Someone cut this tire, Harper. Probably while you were standing by the lake."

A new chill came over her, and she glanced at the pristine forest around her. Was Billy hiding in these woods, watching her? Was he waiting to attack? Trying to lure her into his web so he could watch as she helplessly anticipated his arrival?

Luke rose to his full height, and his hand went to the gun at his waist. He scanned the area, obviously looking for a sign of anything suspicious.

Harper followed his gaze, her senses soaking in everything around them again, looking for a sign of anything she'd missed.

A bird sang. A breeze tickled the branches, clacking them together. Dry leaves brushed against the ground as the wind sent them scattering. Even the leaves were smart enough to listen, which was more than Harper could say for herself at the moment.

"You think . . . you think the killer did this?" Harper hardly wanted to ask the question. Yet she had no choice. She had to know.

"I don't have any better guesses."

"But . . ." Harper had nothing. She wanted to argue. But the evidence was as clear as day.

Someone had been out here with her. And he'd sent another message. A message that clearly indicated he was in control.

"We'll get your tire fixed later," Luke said. "For now, you're coming with me."

"Coming with you? Are you for real?"

"I can't very well leave you stranded out here with

a killer on the loose. Like I said, another murder would be bad PR for the area."

"Aren't you charming?" Harper narrowed her eyes.

"Just get in." He softened his tone. "Please."

She didn't argue this time but climbed into Luke's SUV. Though she'd ridden in it last night, she'd been too distressed to notice much about it.

But now that she was thinking fairly clearly, she noted how neat the vehicle was. Faint tinges of Luke's cologne wafted in the air—a leathery scent that was pleasant. Very pleasant.

A few moments later, Luke took off down the road, his SUV bouncing over the lane.

She stared out the window as they drove, noticing they weren't heading back into town. "Where are we going?"

"I just need to make a quick stop. You can stay in the truck."

"Is it pertaining to the case?"

Luke stared straight ahead. "I can't tell you that."

"I take that as a yes."

"Don't make too many assumptions," he warned. "I am questioning someone who was seen arguing with Tom Brock. But I'm only questioning him. I'm not throwing out any accusations."

"I'm not an enemy, you know." Why was this man so hostile toward her? Harper just didn't get it. She could sense him bristle every time she asked a question.

"You're a reporter. I know how reporters operate, and I know I have to tread with caution. I'd be a fool not to."

"I'm not even writing a story. I'm honestly here just to help." Why was that so hard for Luke to understand?

"Sorry. In my experience as a law enforcement officer, you should never trust a reporter." His jaw flexed with stubborn determination.

He wasn't changing his mind—because he didn't want to change his mind. As far as he was concerned, he'd already closed the case on Harper, and the outcome was that she was someone he should stay away from.

"Well, I'm sorry your experiences have taught you that. Because we're on the same side. The side of justice."

"No, reporters want to get the story. They want the fame that comes with being a part of breaking news—even if they haven't fact-checked anything. All they care about is ratings and bylines."

She crossed her arms. "Not me."

"Pardon me if I don't stick around long enough to find out."

Harper let out a quick breath. This man had a lot of nerve. She really didn't care if she saw Luke again while she was here. She could do what she needed to do without his help.

After shifting into Low to climb the steep mountain road, farther into the heart of the wilderness,

Luke finally pulled to a stop. He put the Explorer into Park and turned toward Harper. "Stay here. Understand?"

"I understand." Her voice was tight with offense. She wished it wasn't, but there was no need to be fake here. Luke had gotten under her skin . . . again.

He climbed out and walked toward the rundown shack with that arrogant swagger. He acted like he was the quarterback in the Super Bowl of life. Men like that . . . she couldn't stand them. Gone was the soft side of Luke that Harper had seen last night.

She didn't know which side was real. Or maybe they both were.

If there was one thing she'd learned from Joe it was that police officers could be master manipulators. They could change from good cop to bad cop in order to get the results they desired.

Was that what Luke was doing? Was he changing his persona in order to find answers? In order to try to deal with her?

As she waited, Harper glanced at her surroundings. Not only was the house in the distance badly neglected, there was trash all over the property. Stacks of wood between trees. Projects that looked like they'd been started and abandoned. Two old cars up on cinder blocks.

She hated to say it, but this place looked like the stereotypical redneck mountain home.

Suddenly, a sound sliced through the air.

Harper's heart stuttered out of control.

Gunfire, she realized.

That was gunfire.

And it was coming from the house in the distance.

Her gaze swerved back to Luke.

She sucked in a quick breath as she saw the sheriff fall to the ground.

106

Chapter Twelve

LUKE DOVE TO THE GROUND, gripping his gun in his hands. That bullet had skimmed his arm—only grazing the skin. But still.

What in the world was Benny thinking?

Was this a sign of his guilt? Had he killed Tom Brock?

Luke glanced back at his Explorer in time to see Harper duck out of sight. Thank goodness. The last thing he needed was for a civilian to get hurt right now.

Quickly, he called for backup. Then he turned his attention back to the shack in the distance.

"Benny, it's me," Luke called. "Sheriff Wilder. Put down your weapon!"

Another shot whizzed past Luke, splintering the tree behind him.

Luke bit back a sharp word.

Nothing was ever easy, was it?

"What are you doing up here?" Benny called.

"I just have a few questions."

"Well, I don't have any answers. Go home."

Irritation rushed through Luke as he repositioned himself on the crisp leaves covering the ground. "Put the gun away, Benny."

"No, I don't wanna. I want you to go home."

Luke was going to have to do this the hard way. "Did you have an argument with Tom Brock yesterday?"

"Who?"

His irritation grew. "You know who Tom Brock is, Benny."

"Why would I argue with him?"

"Because he was going to publish something about you."

"There ain't nothing to publish about me."

"Probably about how you're making moonshine out in the woods behind your house." Benny thought he was being so secretive when, in reality, everybody in town knew about this side business.

Another shot splintered the tree behind him. "I got no idea what you're talking about."

"Did you kill Tom Brock?"

Silence.

Benny didn't know, did he? He hadn't heard Tom was dead. It was the only thing that would quiet the man.

"I'm many things, but I ain't a killer," Benny finally said.

"Then why don't you put the gun down so we can talk?"

Just then, Dewey and Cruise pulled up together. Thankfully, they hadn't been too far away.

Backup had arrived.

Maybe they could put an end to this ridiculous shootout.

"Are you okay?" Harper's heart still raced out of control as Luke climbed back into his SUV.

She'd watched everything from the window, but she hadn't dared get out. She knew better than to do that.

But there had been one moment when she'd honestly thought Luke was dead. She'd seen him go down. But apparently, he'd just dropped to the ground to protect himself.

"Yeah, I'm fine," Luke mumbled.

He didn't sound fine. He sounded cranky. Really cranky.

Rather than letting on about how worried she'd been, Harper shrugged. "I never knew being a small-town sheriff was so exciting."

Luke scowled again. "Yeah, neither did I. While my guys are wrapping up here, I need to get you back into town."

As he put his vehicle in Reverse, Harper saw the blood on his shirt. Even though one of his deputies had helped Luke bandage his arm, concern still ricocheted through her. Without thinking, Harper reached out to touch the area around his wound.

What are you doing?

A jolt of self-consciousness rushed through her, and she pulled her hand back.

Do not touch the sheriff.

Instead, she asked, "Are you sure you're okay?"

After all, Luke had gotten hit by a bullet. Yet he hadn't let that stop him from doing what needed to be done.

Maybe, just maybe, there were times when it was good to have the quarterback around.

"I'm a little bruised, but I should be fine." Luke shifted again and pulled away from the scene.

Harper looked back and saw Benny being led from his house in handcuffs.

She swallowed hard, realizing how ugly this could have turned. Thankfully, everything had ended up okay. "Did you find out what you needed to know, at least?"

"It appeared this was a false lead. Benny had no idea Tom was dead."

Disappointment bit at her. "So the shoot-out was for nothing?"

"The shoot-out was for nothing."

Harper leaned back in her seat, her mind racing. "There's got to be a way to find answers."

"Well, today, most investigations depend on DNA

and trace particles. In this case, we don't have any of those things."

"Almost like a ghost is behind the crimes." A chill rushed through her as she said the words.

Luke did a double take. "This was no ghost."

"I know it wasn't. It just seems like a ghost. I mean, everyone leaves behind evidence, right?"

"Usually."

"How could someone not leave anything behind?"

"That's what we're trying to figure out."

Out the window, trees blurred past, as well as a hand-painted sign advertising apple cider donuts. "What about Tom? Any updates on what happened to him?"

Luke shook his head, no sign of cracking. "I can't tell you that."

"Can you at least tell me if he was murdered or not?"

"No, I can't."

Harper sighed and glanced out the window again. She'd expected as much but hoped for more.

The rest of the ride was silent as they pulled back into town.

But as Luke turned the corner toward the sheriff's office, Harper's eyes widened when she saw a mob of people outside. Most held either a microphone or camera.

"What in the . . . ?" Luke muttered.

He hit the brakes, and his gaze turned toward her. "Did you call the press?"

"Why would I call the press? I'd want to keep the story for myself—not that I'm here to work."

"Someone called the press." Luke's face reddened. "And now I have another mess to take care of."

Luke parked his Explorer, and a sense of trepidation fell over him as he walked toward the crowd surrounding the sheriff's office.

As soon as the mob of reporters saw him, they pointed their microphones and cameras his way, swarming him there on the sidewalk.

"Sheriff, can you tell us about the murders here in Fog Lake?"

"Do you have any suspects?"

"Are residents safe?"

"Are you still going to have the Fog and Hog Festival here this weekend?"

Luke wanted to ignore all the questions. Wanted to keep walking. To pretend like he hadn't heard them.

But he knew that would never fly.

Instead, he paused and scanned the faces in the crowd. Luke halfway expected to spot Harper within the mob, extending a digital recorder toward him with eagerness in her gaze. But she'd disappeared.

He wished he'd taken time to prepare a statement. But he hadn't. Luke had been too busy trying to find a killer.

"I realize why you're all here," he started, praying he would find the right words. "You're looking for a good story. There's no good story to be found here. We've had a tragedy in our town, and authorities here are doing everything within our power to find the person or persons responsible. I'll release other information as I'm able."

"So, Sheriff, you're saying it is safe to be here?" another reporter asked.

Luke contemplated his words. He couldn't tell people it was safe. There was a possible serial killer on the loose. But if he told people it wasn't safe, then he'd cost townspeople their income. He'd cost them the means to buy groceries to feed their children and money to pay their mortgage, to keep their electric on.

There was no winning in this situation.

"I have no comment about that at this time," he finally said.

As Luke turned to walk into the building, another flood of questions sounded behind him. Luke's lungs tightened with tension.

He had to get to the bottom of these murders.

And that meant that he may need to give Harper's theory a little more consideration. He needed to look into Billy Jennings more. He needed to find out if the man had really died.

He also needed to continue looking for Shirley Cue. Whoever the woman was, she'd interacted with the man who'd lured Harper to that apartment. She appeared to be a ghost right now, but someone somewhere knew something.

That also meant he might have to pay another visit to Harper. Because, right now, he had nothing else to go on.

———

Harper's head was pounding when she walked into Hanky's. The restaurant was more of a bar than what she preferred, but she couldn't bring herself to go back to the Hometown Diner right now. Not after her encounter with Shirley Cue yesterday. The scent of alcohol and the dim lighting inside the place nearly made her turn around.

There was only one free seat in the bar area, so Harper took it. She was hungry, and she just needed to be away from Luke for a while. The man had rubbed her the wrong way one too many times.

The woman in the seat beside her glanced her way as Harper ordered a Coke. Harper had noticed her as soon as she walked in—anyone would notice her. The woman was gorgeous, with blonde hair cut into a sharp, chin-level wedge. She had long, thin legs and an overall presence that demanded attention.

"You sure you don't want something stronger?" the woman asked, glancing over as Harper took a sip of her Coke.

Harper lifted her glass. "It's only lunchtime. And, I don't drink, so no."

"Have it your way. But you look like you just saw our town's killer yourself."

Harper let out a puff of air as she remembered the events of the past two days. "No, it was worse. I saw the town's sheriff."

The woman's eyes sparkled. "Luke? You got off to a bad start, huh?"

"You could say that. I don't even know the man, and he hates me."

"Don't take it personally. He's like that with a lot of people."

"You sound like you know." What was this woman's story? Had she dated Luke or something?

"Yeah, I do. I really do." The woman shrugged. "He's been through a lot. Lost his dad six months ago, and he's had a lot of responsibilities to bear since then. I don't think he ever saw himself coming back here."

"That does sound like a lot." Harper figured there was more to his story, but she had no idea what.

"Basically, everyone in this town thinks it's his personal responsibility to take care of this place. He has to keep the streets safe. If things go south, this town shuts down again."

"Again?"

"There used to be a paper mill here about forty years ago. The company decided to close, and everyone lost their jobs. It was close to becoming a ghost town. But about ten years later, tourism started booming. People wanted to come to get away from it all. It revived the town. But if there's a killer on the loose, all of that is in jeopardy. It's a big burden to carry."

"I can imagine." Harper rubbed the side of her glass.

"I'm surprised you haven't run yet," The woman glanced at her again. "Most of the single women have, and I can't blame them."

"You haven't run either."

"Well, I live here. No one's going to drive me away."

"Good for you."

"You still didn't tell me why you're here."

Harper shrugged, wondering how much she should say. "I came to help. But no one wants my help."

"Your help? Are you volunteering to help find the killer? You some kind of profiler or something?"

Harper clamped her mouth shut for a minute. Telling people in town that the killer might be her brother didn't seem like a great idea—not if she wanted anyone to be on her side. "No, but I have some experience."

"And when you say no one wants your help, you mean Luke?"

Harper nodded. "I mean Luke."

The woman shrugged and turned back to her drink. "Give him time. He's slow to warm up. But once you get past his tough exterior, he's like a teddy bear."

Harper threw the woman a skeptical look.

She shrugged. "What? He is. I mean, not exactly a soft, cuddly teddy bear. More like a prickly one. But he's got some squishiness to him, despite that."

"You sound like you know."

The woman glanced at her. "I should. I guess I should introduce myself. My name is Ansley Wilder, and Luke is my big brother."

Chapter Thirteen

"WHEN EVERYTHING GOES south in this town, just let it be known that it's Luke Wilder's fault."

Harper swerved her head toward the loud voice and saw that a man had stepped into the bar. He was large with a lumberjack-style sleeveless flannel shirt, a bushy beard, and an angry disposition. Very angry.

As everyone turned toward him, he nodded at a TV in the corner.

"Turn it up, Walter, so everyone can listen," the man said.

Harper, nearly mesmerized by the scene unfolding around her, turned toward the screen, knowing she wouldn't be able to look away. She sucked in a deep breath when she saw Luke on the air, microphones thrust in his face.

Reporters surrounded him. Based on Luke's expression, he wasn't happy as he turned to address their avalanche of questions.

Harper held her breath and waited to hear what Luke said. Maybe she should have stayed at the scene earlier. Tried to help him.

But he would have never accepted her assistance anyway.

"I realize why you're all here," Luke started. He looked—and sounded—tense but professional. "You're looking for a good story. There's no good story to be found here. We've had a tragedy in our town, and authorities here are doing everything within our power to find the person responsible. I'll release other information as I'm able."

Okay, that was a good, generic start.

Harper let out a breath. Maybe it wasn't that bad.

"So, Sheriff, you're saying it is safe to be here?" a reporter asked.

Luke didn't say anything for a moment, and, again, Harper held her breath. The man was between a rock and a hard place, and she felt for him. Certainly he wanted to keep people safe. But how did he balance that with keeping the town alive?

"I have no comment about that at this time," he finally said.

Her stomach sank. People usually said that when they were hiding something.

People would take that to mean they weren't safe.

"When this town dies, then you look to that there interview for the reason why," Lumberjack man continued.

"Oh, back off and stop being such a jerk,"

Ansley snapped back. "What do you want him to do? To tell everyone this is Mayberry and they can sleep with their doors unlocked and their windows open?"

"No, but he shouldn't be scaring people off, Ansley," the man retorted.

"He's not scaring people off. A killer is, so get over yourself."

The man stormed up to Ansley, but the woman hardly flinched.

Was that alcohol in her system giving her some liquid courage?

Harper braced herself, contemplating what to do. Step in? Let Ansley handle it herself? The woman seemed perfectly capable of doing just that.

The man briefly glanced at Harper, as if sizing up whether or not she was an enemy as well. A flash of something crossed his gaze. Recognition?

Harper wasn't sure.

"Your brother better watch out. Your father would have never started trouble in this town."

"No, your father did that when he ran off with my mother, didn't he?"

The man's eyes lit with anger, and he drew his arm back, like he might throw a punch. Before he could, two other men stepped in and held him back. They dragged him away, but he still muttered curses.

Harper let out a deep breath and turned to the woman beside her. "You've got some guts."

She shrugged. "That's Danny Axton. He's a bully.

I went to school with him. He didn't scare me then, and he sure as the dickens doesn't scare me now."

"Good for you." Maybe. On one hand, Ansley had been incredibly brave. On the other, that bravery might get her hurt.

"What's his stake in all this?" Harper swirled her ice in her glass.

"He's the organizer for the Fog and Hog Festival."

"I see." Harper set her glass down and absently rubbed the sides as she contemplated her next question. "Did your mom really. . .?"

She couldn't bring herself to finish the question. It wasn't her business. She should have never brought it up.

"Yep," Ansley said with more gusto than necessary. "She left my father right after he was diagnosed with cancer the first time. A real winner, huh? And I've got her blood in me. Lucky me."

"I'm sorry." Harper couldn't imagine what that might have been like.

"Another drink, please!" Ansley raised her glass.

"You sure that's a good idea?" Harper asked, knowing it was none of her business yet unable to stop the words.

"Yep. More than sure." Ansley stared straight ahead in stubborn determination as the bartender refilled her drink.

"You know, out of all the people I've met, no one's ever told me they wished they'd drunk more. But many have told me they wished they'd drunk less."

Ansley rolled her eyes. "You sound like my brother."

"Your brother is a smart man."

"I know what I'm doing." She raised her glass again and took a long sip.

"I hope that's true," Harper muttered. "I really do."

Harper took one last look at Danny Axton. He hadn't left the restaurant but sat in the corner glowering.

She remembered Paige's words. About how Billy didn't look anything like he used to. How he'd grown up. Maybe he'd had plastic surgery.

Could Danny Axton be Billy?

It seemed like a long shot. But, until she knew something for sure, she needed to keep an open mind.

"Ansley, you said you grew up with Danny. Does that mean he's always lived here?"

She shrugged. "He did up until he was ten or so. Then his mom left, and he went with her. No one heard from Danny for a long time until he came back here about a year or two ago and took the job with his dad's management company. Their company has been organizing this Fog and Hog Festival for two decades now."

Harper nodded, processing what she'd heard.

She was going to keep Danny Axton on her short list, along with her neighbor Ian.

Just as Harper started toward the stairway to head up to her room at the hotel, a woman came running out from the office.

"Ms. Jennings! Ms. Jennings! I was hoping to catch you." It was the clerk who worked the front desk. Martha.

She stopped beside Harper, huffing and blowing as she tried to catch her breath.

"Is everything okay?" Concern rose in Harper. What reason could this woman possibly have for tracking her down unless something bad had happened.

"Yes. Well, no." Martha let out a nervous laugh. "You see, we just found out that the entire top floor of the motel needs to be treated for bedbugs. We're going to have to move you."

"Bedbugs? Oh, no. I'm sorry to hear that." Harper's skin already felt itchy at the thought.

"Me too. We don't know that there were any in your room, but it's just our protocol to clean the surrounding areas as well."

"Makes sense. Can I just get a different room?"

Martha laughed nervously again. "Well, you see, that's the thing. We had a bunch of vacancies with people fleeing the town and whatnot. But then news of what was going on around here caught wind. Reporters flooded in this afternoon, and now we're booked solid."

Harper shifted her weight. "What are you saying? That I have nowhere to go?"

"Well, no. Not exactly. You see, we have this motel here at the Whistling Pines. But we also have several cabins." She nodded in the distance.

Harper turned and saw six smallish structures on the edge of the lake.

Her stomach sank. Really?

The woman leaned closer. "It should be safe. The killer usually only strikes once every couple of months. He's probably recharging now."

That didn't make Harper feel better.

"Oh, listen to me. I better not talk to those reporters too much or people really will be running from this town."

"So a cabin is my only option," Harper said. "That's what you're saying, correct?"

Her smile disappeared. "Yes, it is. I'm so sorry. But I'll give you a nice one. Your friend has one too."

Harper froze. "My friend?"

"Yes, the redhead who requested a room beside you, right after you checked in. I saw the two of you talking together . . ."

Harper sucked in a deep breath. Why would Ian request to be close to her?

She wasn't sure, nor did she like any of the conclusions she was drawing.

Chapter Fourteen

LUKE SAT AT HIS DESK, his door closed, and an order issued to disturb him only for emergencies.

He needed a moment to clear his head.

Benny was currently locked up for shooting a police officer.

Shirley Cue remained a ghost.

The reporters continued to gather outside.

Who had leaked the information to them?

He had no idea. But he hadn't handled that press conference as well as he should have. He should have prepared a statement first and been proactive in the matter.

Perhaps he'd gotten spoiled down in Atlanta by working for a large department that handled things like that so he didn't have to.

At the thought of Atlanta, Luke's thoughts swerved back in time to the Rocky Ridge murders.

To this day, that case still haunted him.

There had been six murders, all in a neighborhood called Rocky Ridge Estates. It was an upperclass neighborhood, full of homes that cost nearly a million each. Lawyers, doctors, and business people resided there.

The first murder had seemed random. Maybe someone had broken in to steal something only to awaken the homeowner. The victim had died of a gunshot wound to the chest.

As the investigation continued, they'd realized that nothing had been stolen. But maybe the killer had gotten spooked and left after shooting the homeowner.

Two months later, the same scenario played out. A month after that, it happened again. A month later, again. And it continued until they had six victims, and no suspects.

The whole community was in an uproar—as they should be. The guy breaking in had been good —too good.

But they finally got their first lead. As the officers on the case had been talking things over, they hadn't realized that a reporter had been lingering outside the door. She went to press, declaring a sting operation had been set up and that the killer had been found.

The killer had heard about their plan. Instead of killing another victim, he'd killed a police officer.

All because of that reporter who couldn't keep her mouth shut.

Luke sighed and leaned back in his chair, remembering his dismay over all of it. He felt personal guilt about it, especially since he had spoken with the reporter on a couple of occasions. But not about the case.

No, the woman had befriended him at a coffeeshop. Hadn't shared she was a reporter. No, she'd told Luke that she wrote puzzle books for a living. He'd had no reason to question her.

But that day when she'd overheard the officers' conversation . . . she'd come into the station under the guise of seeing him.

And that put part of the responsibility for the policeman's murder on Luke's shoulders as far as he was concerned.

And it was the reason why Harper set off so many warning bells in his head.

Yet she seemed different. He supposed the best reporters did, though.

Out of curiosity, he picked up his phone. He had two calls to make. The first was to the ME's office in Lynchburg, Virginia, where Billy supposedly died. He had to leave a message.

Next, he found a phone number for Harper's boss at the newspaper and dialed it. Loretta Peters answered a moment later.

"This is Sheriff Luke Wilder in Fog Lake, Tennessee. I'm calling regarding one of your reporters, Harper Jennings."

"Yes. What do you need? Is she in trouble?"

"No, ma'am. I'm trying to verify a few things she

told me, and I wanted to ask if you'd sent her here for an assignment."

"To Fog Lake? You're the town in the news right now, aren't you? No, I didn't send her. But if she's there, she should feel free to try her hand at crime reporting. Maybe I won't fire her."

"Fire her?"

"She's one of those convicted people whose mind you can't change. She canceled an interview with Speaker of the House Lyons in order to take this last-minute trip. Speaker of the House Lyons! I still can't believe she'd do something like this. Most reporters would clear their schedule for this opportunity."

Luke thanked her and ended the call.

At least Harper had been truthful about that. Maybe the woman was honest about her intentions here.

Someone knocked at his door. Ms. Mary cracked it open, an apologetic look on her face.

"Hank called," she started. "Your sister needs a ride home from the bar."

Tension sliced the area between his shoulder blades as he stood. Luke had made Ansley promise that she'd call him if she ever needed help. He couldn't scold her for doing just that.

But he had to wonder when his sister was ever going to learn her lesson and stop trying to drown her sorrows with alcohol, among other things.

Harper had just gotten settled into the cabin—as settled as she could be here on the hunting grounds of a serial killer, at least.

Under ordinary circumstances, she would find the stay cozy. The place was small—just one room with a loft. It had windows along the wall facing the lake and an inviting porch that just begged for early morning coffee in the rocking chairs there.

But Harper had already checked all of the windows twice. Tested the locks on the doors. Devised a way to prop a dining room chair against the door handle for extra protection.

She'd never considered herself paranoid, but she was feeling awfully jittery right now.

For the past hour, she'd researched whether or not plastic surgery could make a person unrecognizable.

And the conclusion from all the articles she read? Yes, it could.

A person could change the shape of their nose. Their chin. Their ears. They could change their hair color. Work on changing their build.

Put it all together, and a person could transform.

Most people would still talk the same way. Have the same mannerisms. But with enough practice and determination, someone could change those attributes also.

Which meant that Harper could be speaking with Billy and have no clue she was.

A phone call distracted her, but she frowned when she saw the name there.

It was her boss, Loretta Peters.

Harper drew in a deep breath before answering. "Hi, Loretta."

"I just talked to someone who mentioned you." The woman always got right to the point.

"Who's that?"

"Sheriff Luke Wilder."

She stared out the window at the lake, realizing with clarity just how far she was away from her life in DC. And she didn't really miss it either. "He called you, did he?"

"Seemed concerned about your mental state. Wanted to verify you were an actual reporter."

"He's just doing his homework, I suppose."

"He said you were in Fog Lake."

"I am."

"I just saw the story about the murders there on the news. You going to cover it?"

"I'm not here to work."

"Maybe you should rethink that. I know you hate covering politics, and you'd rather do crime. This could be your chance."

The words ran through Harper's mind. It would be nice to get out of her current position. But . . . that wasn't why she'd come here.

"Think about it," Loretta said. "When will you be back?"

"I don't know."

"Your sudden leave of absence isn't sitting well."

"I have the days." Harper hardly ever took any

time off. She wanted to be a good worker. A hard worker. Usually that was to her detriment. "And I need a couple more of them."

"Okay. But that's it."

Harper ended the call and glanced at her phone. Well, that hadn't gone well.

Then again, she shouldn't be surprised that Luke was checking on her or that Loretta thought she should sell her soul in order to advance her career and get more headlines.

Another reason why this line of work might not be for her.

With a sigh, she dialed her friend Ann Wilkes's number again. Ann was the one who'd originally heard about what was going on here and had emailed her the details on the murders. Harper had been trying to get in touch with Ann for the past couple of days but hadn't been able to get up with her friend.

As the phone rang and rang, she realized she wouldn't get up with her today, either.

Harper sighed and lowered her phone. As she glanced out the window, she saw a Jeep pull in at the house next door.

Her spine stiffened.

Ian Michaels stepped out of the vehicle, along with his friends.

A surge of anger shot through Harper. Before she could talk herself out of it, she left the cabin and charged toward him. Ian's grin faded when he saw her expression.

"You requested the hotel room next to me?" Harper started.

His skin looked a little paler. "What?"

"Don't play coy. The clerk at the motel told me. But you made it sound like a coincidence."

Ian's friends scattered, leaving him to deal with Harper on his own.

Ian raised his hands. "Look, it's not like that."

"Not like that? Are you The Watcher?"

He turned as white as a ghost. "What? Me? No. Of course not."

"Then what are you doing here, Ian?"

"Look, I thought you were cute. I thought if I had a room beside you, we might run into each other. After you checked in, I requested the switch. That's it. I was just being a stupid guy. I'm not a killer."

"Did you ask for this cabin too? The one beside mine?"

His cheeks reddened this time. "Maybe. Like I said, it was innocent. I just wanted an excuse to get to know you."

"Well, I'm sorry if I don't believe you. But there is a killer out there who just happens to be targeting women who look like me."

"I would never hurt a woman. You've got to believe me. Ask my friends. I'm stupid, yes. Sometimes I flirt too much. But I'm not . . . I'm not The Watcher."

Harper believed him. Maybe she shouldn't. Maybe she was being stupid.

But the man looked honestly flummoxed.

Harper nodded. "I'll give you the benefit of the doubt. But don't do anything else stupid."

"I won't. I promise. I won't even talk to you anymore."

Harper turned on her heel and stormed back to her cabin. She locked the doors and then stood there, trying to collect herself. She really was on edge after everything that had happened. Too on edge.

Make some tea. Sit on the couch. Reflect. You've got this, Harper.

Drawing in a deep breath, she put the kettle on. The hotel had been kind enough to provide an array of coffee and tea—enough to hold Harper over until tomorrow, at least.

Just as she turned the burner on, a loud banging sounded at the door.

She jumped so high that her heart rate could hardly keep up. She glanced around the kitchen, looking for something to grab.

Chapter Fifteen

BEFORE HARPER COULD FIND A WEAPON, a voice cut through the air.

"Harper. It's me. Sheriff Wilder. Can I come in?"

She released her breath, chiding herself for being so tightly wound.

Luke. It was just Luke.

Not Billy.

Not a killer announcing himself.

Just Luke.

"Coming!" she called.

Why in the world was the man stopping here? And how had he found her?

Harper's hands trembled as she scooted the chair out of the way and undid the locks. As she opened the door, she shoved her hands into her jean pockets, trying to conceal her nerves.

But Luke's eyes seemed to go right to her arms, like he could sense just how anxious she was.

As Harper soaked in his imposing figure, she nearly forgot about her unsteady hands. Luke wore his sheriff's uniform—khaki slacks and shirt with a thick brown jacket and a ranger-style hat. His eyes were intelligent and perceptive, his face defined, and his presence—though at times abrasive—offered a strange comfort.

"Sorry to stop by unannounced." He nodded beyond her. "Mind if I come in for a minute? I have a few questions for you."

Harper stepped aside. "Come on in."

Luke stepped onto the wooden floor, his presence filling the room. And, as much as the man had irritated her, something about seeing the look of exhaustion in his gaze made Harper soften. She remembered what Ansley had said, that Luke tried to take care of everyone. But who was taking care of him?

It certainly wasn't Harper's job. Not by any stretch of the imagination. Nor did she ever want the job, for that matter.

Despite that, she asked, "Can I get you some tea?"

The kettle screamed on the stove in response.

Harper flinched again, her hand going over her heart before she let out a nervous laugh.

"Jumpy?" he asked, a hint of amusement in his voice.

"Yeah, maybe just a little." There was no need in denying it. She was on edge, and she didn't see that changing any time soon.

"I'll take some tea. Thank you."

As she poured the hot water into two coffee mugs, Harper glanced over at Luke. "How'd you know where I was?"

"Martha told me."

"Martha?"

"At the front desk at the Whistling Pines."

Of course. Martha. Harper should have known.

"A cabin, huh?" he asked, glancing around.

"It wasn't my first choice."

"I don't blame you. Isn't there somewhere else you could stay?"

"Nope. They're treating the top floor for bedbugs. That's why I had to vacate. All the other rooms are suddenly booked everywhere in town. Reporters may have single-handedly saved the economy in this town, at least for the weekend."

He shrugged nonchalantly. "You could always leave."

"You really want me out of town, don't you?" Harper raised an eyebrow as she gave him a pointed look.

"Just trying to look out for your safety."

She crossed the room and handed him his mug. "Well, I appreciate it, but I'm a big girl. I'll be okay."

She hoped her words were true.

Luke said nothing, only watched her for long enough that she fidgeted.

"Look, would you like to sit on the porch and drink our tea? It is nice outside, and since you're here

. . ." *Since you're here what, Harper?* "I guess it's safe and all."

"Sure thing." Luke didn't smile. That would lighten the moment too much. And Luke obviously took this very seriously.

As he should.

As Harper followed him outside, she reached for the door handle at the same time he did. Their hands brushed, and a jolt of electricity pulsed through her.

What in the world? That was some kind of fluke. The idea of feeling anything toward this man was ludicrous. All Luke had done was doubt her and try to get her to leave. That seemed like an unlikely recipe for being attracted to each other. Yet . . .

They took a seat on the rockers and silently stared out over the lake for several minutes. The steaming tea in her hands was the perfect complement to the misty lake.

Since Luke didn't seem to be in a hurry to get started, Harper said, "I met your sister today."

"Did you? I just came from driving her home." His voice sounded strained.

"Did you? She seems very nice . . . and feisty."

"She is. But she was so intoxicated that the bar owner called me. Apparently, she and Danny Axton were coming to blows."

Harper cringed. "I'm sorry to hear that. I actually experienced part of that confrontation."

"Ansley hasn't taken what life's handed to her very well lately, to put it lightly."

"She said your mom left and your dad died of cancer."

"True on both counts. Our family has been dealt some hard blows." Luke let out a breath and leaned forward. "That's not what I came to talk about."

"No, of course not." Harper straightened. For a moment—and just a moment—she'd felt as if she was talking to a new friend. The thought had been foolish. Of course, Luke was here on business.

"Look, Harper. I should probably get to the point of why I came here." Luke, still leaning forward on his knees, angled his head toward her.

"Okay."

"But first I want to apologize. I misjudged you, and I should have given you more of a chance."

Her eyebrows shot up in surprise. She hadn't expected that. "It's okay. I knew it would sound outlandish."

"We don't have very many leads right now. None of the crime lab reports or the ME conclusions have pointed to any answers. Everyone is on edge. I'm willing to consider any theory at this point."

"What do you want to know about mine?"

"Why can't I find any information about Billy Jennings online?"

Harper let out a long breath and leaned back. Billy. He was such a complicated subject. "Do you have a few minutes?"

"I have as much time as you need right now." He raised his cup. "At least, until I finish this tea."

"Well, drink slowly." Harper rubbed her lips together to prep herself for a dive into her past. It wasn't a place she liked to go and visit very often, if she could help it.

Luke said nothing, just waited.

She crossed her legs in the rocking chair and brought her tea closer. "Billy, as we called him, was found on the streets in downtown Raleigh when he was only ten. He didn't speak. Authorities couldn't figure out his name or what had happened. He was just this little lost boy who needed a home."

"Go on."

"Even though there was a campaign to find out who he was, nothing came from it. He went into foster care, but he lasted less than a year in each home, it seemed. Sometimes, it was only a few days. By the time Billy reached our house when he was sixteen, he'd already been with ten different families."

"That doesn't sound good."

"He was . . . he was troubled."

"What do you mean?"

Harper stared at the rim of her cup, stared at the tea inside, which grew tepid as the cold air surrounded it. Her soul felt similar as the memories invaded her. "Well, he eventually did speak, but he couldn't remember his past or how he got on the streets. He really started coming out of his shell while at our house, and he transformed into a different person."

"The right family can do that."

Harper grimaced. "Billy could be so charming when he wanted to be. His eyes would dance, and his smile was infectious. My mom fell in love with him and thought he was the perfect child, the son she'd always wanted."

"There's a 'but' in there, I'm assuming." Luke glanced at her, the mellow remnants of the sunset casting brilliant shades of light across his features.

If this moment wasn't so tense and fraught with a decade of old pain, it might be picturesque, worthy of a magazine cover or a tourism brochure. Luke could certainly be the poster boy for mountain living.

Men here in the mountains certainly exuded a different kind of manliness than those in DC. Harper preferred this kind of masculinity—rugged, natural. It was refreshing and fascinating, all in one.

Harper cleared her throat, turning her thoughts back to their conversation. "If you don't mind, I need to go back a little further in time even before I can explain."

"Take all the time you need, Harper."

His words sounded surprisingly reassuring, and Harper felt her heartbeat steady under his encouragement. Maybe he wasn't the ogre she'd assumed he was. Maybe he was just a man who was under too much pressure, but he was trying to do the right thing. He was trying to protect the people who depended on him.

Harper licked her lips. It would be nice to have someone so protective. The people of this town,

Luke's family . . . they didn't realize how lucky they were.

She continued. "So, I was the only child my parents were able to have the natural way, so to speak. The doctor actually told my mom she would never have a child, but surprise! I came along. But Mom had always wanted a big family. She'd grown up as an only child, and she'd hated it. Plus, my dad worked in corporate America all the time. All. The. Time. So it was really just my mom and me for the first eight years of my life."

"Okay."

"So my mom decided to become a foster mom, which is a wonderful thing. It really is. And she loved it. It became her life. She fostered seventeen kids and adopted six of them."

"Wow."

"I was always the oldest. Someone advised her not to change the birth order of her biological family, so she listened. But . . . I guess the best way to say it is that she became fanatical about it. She'd always run a tight ship, but it kept getting tighter. A few TV shows began showing some interest in our family, wanting to do a reality show."

"What did your mom think about that?"

"She loved it. She loved attention. Magazine articles were written about her. She was chosen as Woman of the Year. She was asked to be the keynote speaker at adoption symposiums."

"And Billy?"

She let out a long breath. "Billy came to our house when I was nineteen. He was sixteen. And, like I said earlier, my mom was taken with him. Whenever he was around her, he turned on all of his charm and acted like the perfect son."

"But you saw a different side of him?"

The intensity in Harper's gut grew stronger—along with the nausea. "I woke up one night, and he was standing over my bed. With a knife. At first, I thought he was dreaming. I asked him what he was doing."

"And he said?"

"That he was imagining what it would be like to kill me."

Luke's eyes widened. "It must have been terrifying."

"To say the least. I told him to go away, and he smiled, like he'd enjoyed the whole encounter."

"Did you tell your mom?"

"I did. And she didn't believe me." Saying the words caused a fresh wave of betrayal to wash over Harper. All these years, and that realization still hurt. It probably always would.

"Why wouldn't she believe you?"

Harper tried to keep her emotions in check, even though they wanted to roar out of control. But she couldn't let bitterness define her.

"My mom said I was jealous of Billy and trying to get attention."

"But three years ago he found you in DC and did

the same thing—only he actually sliced your throat that time."

"That's right."

Luke didn't show any judgment. He bobbed his head up and down in a slow nod before calmly asking, "Did he ever do the same thing to anyone else in the house?"

"Not that I know of. It became my mission to watch him and make sure he didn't. But his shenanigans grew from there. I'd wake up, and he'd be standing over me, this flute in his hands that my mom had gotten him in Cherokee, North Carolina. He'd blow into it, and he was always working on this song that sounded so sad and eerie. He was . . . well, he was messed up, to say the least."

"How did he get into your room? I'm assuming you locked your door."

Harper shivered. "I did. But he knew how to get around locks. He picked them or something. I guess the last straw was when I woke up one morning, and I had something red smeared on my cheeks."

"Blood?"

She shook her head. "It was red paint. But I think Billy pretended it was blood. It didn't matter. The effect was still the same—total terror."

"You told your mom all of that and she still didn't believe you?"

"Nope. At that time, she was wrapped up in negotiations with this reality TV show. She'd decided to stop fostering, basically because foster kids couldn't be on TV. She'd adopted six kids by then, though."

"Wow."

"Yeah, but she didn't want anything to ruin her chances of being on TV. I told her I wouldn't be a part of it. Not if Billy was in it. I didn't want to pretend to be this perfect family when we weren't."

Luke took another sip of his tea and stared off at the lake. "How did your mom take that?"

The memories pummeled her. Harper didn't like to talk about this part of her life. But she had no choice at the moment. Luke needed to know the whole story. She'd go back in time and relive the most painful moments if it meant stopping the killer.

"My mom said if I didn't cooperate, I had to get out. I told her she was putting the whole family in danger, and that I wasn't going to go along with it. So she kicked me out. I begged to stay—mostly so I could keep an eye on my siblings. But she wouldn't let me. She made up this story about how I'd gone away to college. She hasn't let me into the house since then."

"That's . . . that's harsh."

"It was. But, in the end, the reality show didn't happen—that was a good thing."

"I'd say so."

Harper turned toward him. "I know that was a long story. But you deserve to know everything. I know my mom planted doubts in your mind. And I know it has to be perplexing why Billy doesn't exist online. The truth is, he probably changed his name, just like he changed his appearance when he left. Deceit comes easily to him."

"I'm in the process of checking the accident and death reports in the county where you said his accident took place." Luke shifted forward. "A couple things here. You said, Billy left. When was that, and how do you know about it?"

"I keep up with my siblings. They told me he left about three years after I was kicked out. He disappeared, basically. Unfortunately, it's not all that uncommon with kids who have been in the system. And with his history . . . well, you know."

"Your mom said she talked to him about a year ago. That must have been right before the accident."

"My guess is that they called each other on occasion. Or, more likely, Billy called her whenever he needed something."

"And you also said he changed his appearance?"

"When I talked to my sister Paige earlier she said last year she ran into an old friend who'd seen Billy and told her he looked different."

"Different how?"

"We're not sure except his hair was red. I asked Paige to call Shari and find out more details. I haven't heard back yet."

"So what you're saying is that Billy, if he's still alive, could be staring you in the face, and you might not even know it?"

A shiver went down Harper's spine. "Yes, that's exactly what I'm saying."

Then she told him about Ian, the redheaded stranger who'd requested a room next to hers at the motel and the cabin.

Could it be nothing? Absolutely. But Harper wouldn't be so foolish as to keep that information to herself.

Chapter Sixteen

LUKE TRIED NOT to stare at Harper as she sat in the rocking chair with the mist roiling behind her. But it was hard. The woman had surprised him.

She was principled. And Luke had so many other questions he wanted to ask her.

Why had she become a reporter? What had happened after she'd been kicked out by her mother? How could she act so calm right now after everything that had happened to her?

But those questions were none of his business.

Only those that pertained to the case were fair game right now, no matter what his desires might tell him.

It had been a long time since someone had captured his attention so quickly like Harper had. Even though he'd felt abrasive toward the woman when they'd first met, maybe it was because his subconscious was telling him to keep his distance.

Something internal told him he had no room in his life for any kind of relationship.

What if that internal urgency wasn't telling him the truth, though? What if it was fear talking?

"So you have no idea why, if this guy is your brother, he might have chosen Fog Lake?" Luke shifted forward in the rocking chair.

Harper shook her head, her curls dancing around her face. "I have no idea. My guess is that it could have something to do with his past, those missing years before he was found on the streets."

"If authorities all those years ago couldn't identify who he was, I doubt it's going to be possible now."

"I would agree." She grimaced, and Luke could see the question forming on her lips. "What do you know about Danny Axton?"

Luke felt his muscles tighten. "He's not my favorite person."

"I heard he left the area for several years."

Luke blinked as he processed those words. "He did. But . . . I don't know. I don't care for the man, but I'm not sure I can see him being responsible for these murders. You think the killer is someone who's already here? A local."

Harper turned, seeming to come alive as she began to dive into her response. Her eyes sparked, her hands rose, and her voice lilted. "Well, think about it. This guy is blending in. If he were a tourist, people would notice the new guy who'd been in town since the killings started. And you're right on in your question about why Fog Lake. Someone has a connection to it. A local makes the most sense."

Luke let out a long breath and ran a hand over his face. "The thought has crossed my mind. I hate to think anyone I know might be responsible."

"But it would be foolish not to consider the possibility."

"Yes, it would be foolish not to consider it. But I don't like the idea of it."

"You're not supposed to. When people you trust do horrible things, it should be shocking and it should make you angry."

Luke hated to admit it, but he was liking Harper more and more all the time. She was one of the first people he'd met since moving back here whom he felt like he could relate to.

When he'd met her two days ago, he would have never thought that would be the case. No, the woman had gotten under his skin. But when he set aside his preconceived notions of who she was, he found himself warming up quickly.

Too quickly.

He glanced at her again, at the way the sun hit her dark hair. At the sincerity in her gaze.

He caught a glimpse of her scar peeking out from her collar and remembered everything she'd been through. Yet she was still here. Still determined to do the right thing.

She seemed to notice him staring and touched her scar, covering it with her hand.

"I didn't mean to make you uncomfortable," he said. "I'm sorry."

"It's okay. It's a part of who I am now, for better or worse."

"I can't imagine what you went through."

"I didn't sleep for months. My boyfriend dumped me because he couldn't handle how the event changed me. And I was angry for a long time. Angry that my mom hadn't listened to me. That she'd chosen Billy over me. Upset because the police hadn't found the person who did this to me."

"I can imagine."

"But then I realized I had to make a choice for my life. I could cower in fear and resentment, or I could take what had been handed to me and make the best of it."

"And you decided to make the best of it."

She offered a soft smile. "That's the goal."

Luke turned back to the lake, trying to keep his thoughts focused—on the case.

Harper had given him a lot to think about. Maybe Luke should examine some locals a little more closely. Had any of them been gone from the area for an extensive amount of time?

It was hard to say. And, quite frankly, Luke had been gone from the area for twelve years when he worked as a detective in Atlanta. He was entering dangerous territory if he started pointing the finger at anyone who fit the description.

So he wouldn't point fingers. But he would consider all the possibilities.

Harper's phone rang, and she excused herself to answer. He listened to the conversation—though one-sided—as he heard her voice grow tense.

Something was wrong.

He braced himself for whatever might be going on—if Harper decided to share any details with him. Did it have to do with this case? That was his guess.

When Harper hung up, she turned toward him. The animated look was gone, and stoic fear replaced it.

The bad feeling in his gut grew.

"That was my sister Paige," Harper started. "She called someone about her friend Shari. Shari lives about five hours away, and the two of them only talk a couple times a year. Shari is the one who saw Billy about a year ago, right before his accident, and said he looked different."

"And?"

Harper swallowed hard. "And Shari hasn't been heard from since then. No one has seen her."

Harper felt colder than she'd like as she climbed the ladder into the loft to try and get some sleep. The space wasn't fancy, but it was sufficient. A mattress on the floor had a cozy quilt tossed over it. A small night-stand sat to one side with a little lamp on it.

And that was it. But, as she glanced out from the loft, she had a view of the entire cabin, and the lake gleamed on the other side of the windows.

Harper sighed. She still had so much she wanted to do. She needed to find more answers.

But those things would have to wait until tomorrow. Right now Harper needed sleep, a commodity that would be hard to come by with all the thoughts racing through her mind.

As she turned over in her bed, her mind went to Luke again. He'd surprised her tonight by being a good listener. By showing compassion. By not seeming so prickly, she supposed.

Their talk had almost felt pleasant, other than the subject matter.

Still, Harper was thankful she'd been able to tell Luke her side of the story. And he actually might believe her. Some of the doubt had left his gaze.

He'd even left her with his cell phone number, just in case she needed anything.

It had been thoughtful.

And totally professional.

She chuckled, chiding herself. Of *course* it was just professional. And, even if it wasn't, it wouldn't matter. Harper didn't want to marry or date anyone in law enforcement. Nope, she wanted someone with a nine-to-five job who could also be a family man.

She turned over again on the lumpy mattress, and her leg hit the vent cover beside her, causing it to fall off and clatter to the floor. She'd mused earlier that it was an odd place to put the return vent for the HVAC system.

With a sigh, Harper sat up, grabbed the metal cover, and tried to secure it back onto the three-by-three-foot opening. When the grate was secure, she lay down again, determined to get some sleep.

Her gaze went across her dark cabin to the lake. The beautiful lake.

Sometimes, glimpses of moonlight would cut through the fog and illuminate the gentle ripples in the water. Sometimes she could see hints of the mighty forest across the lake. Other times it looked like a twister had picked up the cabin and dropped it in the middle of a scene from a scary movie.

Only special effects could produce so much atmosphere.

But this fog was no special effect.

Harper pulled the blanket closer, unable to draw her gaze away from the view.

It was too bad a madman had ruined this experience for so many.

It was too bad Billy had ruined it.

She frowned. Could Harper really be this certain that Billy was behind this? Part of her wanted to be 100 percent confident. But part of her doubted her theory. Sure, the man fit the basic description of the killer. But there were still too many unknowns to say for sure.

Harper blinked as something in the distance

caught her eye. Was that . . . a person outside, in front of her cabin?

No. Her eyes were playing tricks on her. No one was out there watching her. She'd been seeing things.

Still, Harper's heart pounded harder.

It's the power of suggestion. You've been thinking about the horror of seeing a figure in the middle of the fog, and now you think you see thus-said figure.

But when Harper blinked, the figure reappeared.

There *was* a man out there.

A man.

In the fog.

Watching her.

A scream caught in Harper's throat.

It was The Watcher.

He was here.

And Harper was his next target.

Terror raced up and down her bones, her spine, her muscles.

She had to do something.

The man had been close. Nearly on her porch.

By the time she scrambled down the ladder and escaped outside, he'd catch her. That would never work.

Her phone.

That was right.

Harper's hands shook so badly she nearly dropped the device. But she managed to dial Luke's number.

Please answer. Please answer.

Harper glanced back up and blinked. The man

was gone. Her lungs were so tight she could hardly breathe. Where had he gone? How was he planning to get inside?

Oh, dear Lord. Please help me.

"Hello," Luke said, his voice sleepy.

"It's me." Harper's voice cracked. "The man. He's outside my cabin."

"I'll be right there, Harper." His voice zinged, like adrenaline had pushed away any of his grogginess. "Is there anywhere you can hide?"

She glanced around. There was nowhere to go.

Except . . .

"Maybe," she whispered.

"Then get there. Now. I'm on my way. Only five minutes from your place. Hang on. Do you understand?"

But before Harper could answer, she heard a squeak.

Her door had opened.

The man was inside her cabin.

Chapter Seventeen

HARPER DIDN'T HAVE much time to move.

And she had to be quiet.

Very quiet.

Otherwise, she would die.

Keeping the blanket close to mask any noise, she scooted toward the vent. With trembling hands, she pried the metal square from its frame. Holding it to the side, she stuffed a blanket inside to mute any noise and then slid into the opening.

Despite her quakes, Harper managed to pull the cover back on.

And then she tried to catch her breath.

Each inhale and exhale sounded so heavy that she was sure the intruder could hear. But Harper couldn't control it. Fear pulsated out of control in her body.

Would the man find her in here?

Would Luke get to the cabin in time?

Was this the way Harper would die? With a slash

across her neck—one that would prevent her from screaming for help?

A cry caught in her throat at the thought.

Harper had always thought she didn't fear dying. But Harper had been wrong. Now that death lingered close enough to touch, terror raced through her blood.

Her panting still sounded heavy. Too heavy.

Certainly the man would hear her. Her exhalations would be like the telltale heart.

She had to stay silent.

Harper squeezed her eyes shut and willed herself to calm down.

I could use a little help here, Lord. Please. I can't do this on my own.

When Harper opened her eyes, she stared between the slats of the vent. Finally, images from the other side came into focus—though barely. What she could see made her skin crawl.

A man casually paced her cabin, almost like he was checking it out as a real estate investment. He went to the bookcase and perused the items there.

He was so . . . relaxed.

Another shiver went down Harper's spine.

It was too dark to make out his features.

Was it Billy?

Harper couldn't be sure.

The intruder seemed in no hurry as he glanced around, taking things in. She watched as he picked up the tea cup Harper had drunk out of earlier and examined it.

What . . .?

He hasn't seen you yet, Harper. Not yet. Maybe he won't.

That didn't stop her heart from thumping out of control.

How had this guy gotten inside? She couldn't make sense of it. Harper hadn't heard a thing. And she'd locked the door. Used the deadbolt. Used the safety chain.

The man began moving again. Her ears rang as her blood pressure surged.

He sauntered.

Toward the loft.

Toward her.

Harper held back a cry as panic invaded every part of her.

How long would it take him to figure out where she hid?

No, he wouldn't. Don't think like that. Luke will arrive first.

A creak stretched through the air. The sound made terror travel up her spine again.

Her lungs froze. Gone were her worries about being too loud with every intake and exhale of air. Now she might pass out from lack of oxygen.

The wood groaned again under the intruder's weight.

He was getting closer.

How much time had passed?

Minutes ticked by, each one feeling like an hour.

How far away had Luke said he was? Five minutes?

If Harper's estimations were right, he should be here at any time.

But it might still be too late.

She swallowed a cry of despair.

Harper wasn't ready to die. Not yet. No, there were so many things she wanted to experience. Things she needed to change.

She imagined the other victims. Had they thought the same thing? Had they felt this same panic?

She willed herself not to move. Not to do anything to give away where she was.

The blanket, Harper realized, startling.

Had she gotten all the material inside the shaft?

She glanced down and held back a gasp.

One of the corners hung out. She tugged at it, but the blanket wouldn't budge. If she pulled too hard, the vent cover might fall off again.

No, no, no!

Harper jerked her gaze back toward the man.

Slowly and methodically, his shadow rose as he climbed into the loft.

Balanced on his knees.

Stood.

Be useful. Get a good look at him. Just in case you survive this.

Harper squeezed the blanket beneath her, fighting panic.

Then she squinted. She wanted—needed—to see what this man looked like. But it was still too dark. Harper could only make out a masculine figure with a stocking cap and black clothing.

This man could be anyone.

"Harper." His whisper floated across the air like a deadly poison. "I know you're here."

Her skin nearly crawled right off of her.

He was close. Too close.

Close enough to reach her in five seconds.

The man's hand went to his pocket, and he reached for something. A knife?

Was this it?

Instead, the haunting tone of a Native American flute filled the air.

Each blow of the pipe wound her nerves tighter and tighter.

Harper squeezed the blanket again.

Stay still. Whatever you do, don't move.

"Sounds nice, doesn't it?" the man whispered again. "Like a war cry."

Did that voice belong to Billy? She couldn't be sure.

He took a step toward her, toward the vent, but froze.

Another sound rumbled in the distance.

A car. A car had pulled up on the gravel lane by her cabin.

Harper's heartrate surged. Luke? Was it Luke? Would he get to her in time?

Or would this man finish what he'd come to do?

As the intruder stepped toward her again, Harper's blood turned ice cold.

He was going to kill her, wasn't he? And nothing would stop him.

———

Luke reached Harper's cabin, threw his SUV into Park, and rushed out. As he sprinted from his car, he drew his gun.

He paused on the porch long enough to collect himself—only a split second—and then Luke threw his body weight into the door. The wood splintered before bursting open.

Luke caught his breath and stared inside the dark house.

Where was this guy? What had he done? Had Luke gotten here in time?

He pushed away the questions and stepped inside.

He scanned the interior.

He saw nothing.

Heard nothing.

Where was the man?

"Luke, watch out!" someone screamed.

Before he could turn, something came down hard on his head. As he went to his knees, a figure came into view, standing over him.

The Watcher?

Was that The Watcher?

Luke had to get him. But his body didn't cooperate. And his head—it pounded as he fought to remain lucid. He couldn't give in. No, Harper needed him.

Luke tried to push himself up. But the room wobbled around him, and he let out a groan.

In the next instant, Harper appeared beside him. Her voice sounded breathless as she asked, "Luke, are you okay?"

"Yeah," he muttered, knowing better than to nod his head.

But the important thing was that Harper was okay. She was alive. Safe.

"I'm glad you're okay." What was the edge Harper had in her voice?

Luke grasped his temple, trying to think clearly.

Before he could, Harper grabbed his gun. "Luke, I'm sorry."

"Sorry about what?"

She frowned. "I'll be back."

Luke drew in a sharp breath when he realized what she was doing. She was going after this guy. He couldn't let her do that. Yet his body wouldn't move.

"Harper—"

Before he could argue, she darted out the door.

Chapter Eighteen

LUKE LET OUT A GROAN.

What was the woman thinking?

He pushed himself to his feet, suddenly feeling more alert. He had no choice but to be. As he staggered onto the porch, he spotted Harper standing by the lake, gun drawn, and her gaze jerking from left to right as she looked for the intruder.

No one else was in sight.

But Harper looked wired and ready to shoot anything that moved.

The night felt taut with tension, like nature had picked up on their fear and waited with bated breath to see what might happen.

"Harper," he called.

She veered toward him, gun still drawn.

Luke sucked in a deep breath and walked toward her.

He wanted to reprimand her for being irresponsible. But the distress in her gaze silenced him.

The woman was terrified but determined to put an end to this.

Harper's bones looked like they turned to jelly when she saw him, and she let out a cry. Luke caught her elbow before she collapsed to the ground.

"I thought I could catch him," she whispered, her voice cracking as she rasped in shallow breaths.

"It's okay, Harper."

Tears pushed at her eyes, but she said nothing else. Luke's heart ached when he saw her brutal determination. There were too many emotions on Harper's face to fully comprehend them all. But he worried she might go into shock.

"Come on," Luke said, glancing around one more time. "Let's get you back inside."

Harper didn't argue as he led her into the cabin and to a couch. He flipped the lights on and glanced around before joining her.

"Are you okay?" Luke studied her face, unsure about everything that had played out here tonight.

She nodded, her face almost blank. But the telltale tears at the corners of her eyes made it clear she hadn't checked out. No, she was feeling everything on an internal level.

"I'm going to make sure everything is clear. Okay?" Luke said the words slowly, trying to make sure she understood.

She nodded again.

Hesitantly, Luke stepped away and pulled out his

phone. He needed his deputies here. He needed them to search for the man responsible. They needed to comb this place for evidence as well.

Luke didn't have to go very far.

He paused by the bookshelf, where a basket of pinecones, a wood figure of a bear, and pictures from the mountains—landscape views, cozy cabins, a deer —stared back.

On the bottom shelf, there was a picture. A loose picture.

Of a family. A man and woman surrounded by seven kids. Slipping a glove on, Luke picked up the photo.

One of the faces had an X over it, crudely added with a red marker.

Luke would need to confirm with Harper, but he felt certain the picture was of Harper and her family.

Harper pulled the blanket closer around her shoulders. She wasn't even sure who had put the blanket around her, but she was grateful for the warmth and comfort it offered. The gas fireplace also helped drive the chill from the air.

Luke had allowed her to stay on the couch as his team continued to search her cabin. But she couldn't get that photo out of her mind. The picture of her family. Of Billy. The one where her face had an X over it.

She heard the officers gathering behind her after they'd searched the house.

"Anything else?" Luke asked.

"No, sir," Deputy Dewey said. "There were a few footprints in the soil near the house that we're guessing belong to either us or the groundskeeper. We'll put them on file, just in case anything else turns up."

"Did you examine the doors?" Luke asked.

Yes, the doors. How had that man gotten inside?

"We did," Dewey said. "It looks like he got in through the back door. He managed to pick the two locks at the bottom, and he used some kind of tool to snap through the chain. Those things are usually pretty flimsy anyway."

"That's a change from his normal MO, though."

"Yes, sir. It is."

Why was that? How had he gotten into the other victim's homes? No, they'd called the police. Yet the killer got into their homes before they'd arrived.

After his deputies left, Luke still remained.

He lowered himself beside Harper and rubbed his head, just as he'd been doing since the man hit him on the head.

Harper winced as she realized that he'd taken a hard blow. Anything with the head was serious business, yet he'd ignored his own concerns to handle this crime scene. "You should get that checked out."

"I'll be fine."

"I'm sorry I grabbed your gun." Guilt pounded at

Harper as she recalled the events from tonight. "I didn't really think. I just reacted. I thought . . . maybe I could catch him and end this."

"You put your life on the line."

"My life is already on the line." Her words—though truthful—sounded dull.

Luke released a breath. "Harper—"

"You know it's true. If you hadn't gotten here when you did, that man would have killed me. He heard your car pull up and decided to retreat instead."

"Did you recognize the man, Harper? The picture indicates that you were right and that it must be Billy behind this. But we can't make assumptions here."

She shook her head. "I wish I did recognize him —more than anything. But it was too dark. I couldn't see anything except a shadowy figure."

Luke said nothing, just stared off in contemplation again.

Harper stood, still keeping the blanket around her. "Let me get you an ice pack for your head at least. And maybe some Tylenol. I think I have some in my bag."

Luke didn't argue.

A few minutes later, she handed him a bottle of water, the pills, and a Ziploc bag full of ice. "This is about as far as my nursing skills go."

"Thank you." Luke took the pills, threw them back in his mouth, and swallowed with no water. He set the ice on the table instead of using it.

Harper could tell his thoughts were heavy and burdensome.

"I don't know how to keep you safe, Harper." His voice sounded tight with barely controlled emotion.

Something about the way he said the words did something strange to her heart. She reached out and touched his arm as she remembered Ansley talking about the extreme pressure he was under right now. "It's not your job."

"But it is. That's what this town hired me to do. Keep people safe."

"I came here of my own free will. I'm staying here of my own free will. Whatever happens to me, it will be because of my choices and because of the killer."

Luke let out a sigh and lowered his head, his shoulders appearing burdened with invisible weights. "That's not good enough."

"It's going to have to be."

He sat silently again before dragging his gaze up to her. "Harper, what brought you here? How did you happen to find out about these murders? Do you have a Google alert set up for something like this?"

She let out a mild laugh. It wasn't funny. It wasn't. Yet, in a twisted, macabre way, Harper supposed it could be.

Her laughter faded quickly as she remembered how it had all come about. She let out a deep sigh, wondering how much she should share. Because, the truth was, she hadn't been looking for this. Instead, she'd stumbled upon it and hadn't been able to look away.

"I actually got an email from a friend of mine." She pulled her legs beneath her, settling in to tell her story. "She was one of the few people I told about Billy. She knew what he'd done. We went to journalism school together, and she took a job for a newspaper out in Roanoke, Virginia. Anyway, she heard what was going on here and sent me an email about it."

"I've been trying to keep the stories quiet, but there were a couple of nearby small-town newspapers that caught wind of what happened," Luke said. "However, some of those details you know about were never released to the press."

"I guess my friend knows someone who frequents this area, so she heard the town's scuttlebutt. Said it wasn't public or confirmed. But as soon as I heard some of those details . . ."

"You dropped everything and came here."

"I was still chewing on the first two murders when I heard about the third. That's when I knew I couldn't just sit back and wonder what was going on. I had to know."

"Makes sense."

"I love fighting for what's right, but I really hate writing about politics. I can't find much that's right with politics, you know?"

"They're pretty messed up most of the time."

"Exactly. I'm not married to my job, and there are

some things in life that are worth sacrificing for."

An unreadable emotion crossed his gaze, and Harper wondered what it was about. Was it admiration? Or maybe Luke thought she was stupid. She really had no idea.

And she didn't really care. What other people thought about her . . . it wasn't really her concern. She only had to answer to herself and her Creator.

Harper suddenly realized that she wasn't that tired, after all. She doubted she'd be getting any rest tonight. Maybe not for a while.

Luke shifted, and a moment of panic raced through her. She couldn't be here alone. Not after what had happened. Yet she knew that Luke couldn't stay.

So she made the decision and stood. "I'm going with you to the sheriff's office."

"What?" Surprise raced through Luke's voice.

"Let's face it. Neither of us are getting any sleep tonight. You need to work, and I'm certainly not going to stop you. So I'll hang out at the station for a while—at least until the sun comes up."

Luke examined her. "You're a surprising woman, Harper Jennings."

"I won't ask if that's a compliment or an insult."

A soft smile feathered his lips. "Oh, it was a compliment. Definitely a compliment."

Harper's chest warmed at his words. Maybe she'd finally broken through the prickly sheriff and had a peek of the supposed teddy bear inside.

Chapter Nineteen

IT HADN'T WORKED out this time.

No, Harper was smart. She'd hidden. She'd called for help.

He'd known she would.

That was why he mostly wanted to scare her.

He thought it had worked.

If anyone had the power to bring him down, it was Harper.

And he couldn't let that happen.

Didn't she know that he was just getting started here? When he stopped and allowed himself to dream about the deepest desires of his heart, he realized that all he wanted was more of this.

Of *this*.

Seeing the fear, it was addictive.

Seeing the life drain from someone, it was addictive.

Seeing that moment of panic in his victims, it was addictive.

And this was the place, the town, where it all had started.

So it seemed only appropriate to come back here. To make not only his victims pay, but to make the town pay as well.

And pay, the town would.

He couldn't wait to see it all go down.

Soon, he told himself.

Soon.

He only hoped he could be patient enough to wait.

And he hoped that sheriff didn't get in his way. He'd seen the way he looked at Harper. He'd seen the curious look in his eyes. The attraction that he tried to fight.

The poor man could use someone to loosen him up.

It was too bad that wouldn't be happening.

The sheriff was going to have to add one more tragedy to an already long list of them in his life.

Chapter Twenty

LUKE GLANCED across his desk and saw Harper. She'd curled into a ball at the edge of the couch in the reception area. She looked so comfortable as she lay there.

A moment of gratitude filled him. Harper had somehow been able to see all the different directions he was being pulled. She'd reached into the situation and come up with a solution.

She'd looked out for . . . him.

The thought shouldn't be so surprising, but it was. Luke had always been the protector. The one who tried to help others. It was a rare day when anyone tried to watch out for his best interests.

Harper Jennings was certainly a surprise.

As he sat there, he thought about her theory. Thought about whether or not this killer might be a local who was hiding in plain sight.

The theory was worth exploring.

Luke pulled out a pad of paper and tried to think of anyone who may have left town around ten years of age. Who might have come back.

Danny Axton came to mind. He'd moved away when his parents divorced and he'd gone with his mom.

The man certainly had a temper.

Yet his job—his family's company—depended on tourism. So for him to be the killer would be a stretch.

But he couldn't rule the man out yet.

Then there was the redhead who'd been Harper's neighbor at the motel. Ian Michaels. Luke would talk to him tomorrow.

Benny had been a suspect, but they'd ruled him out.

Who was he missing?

Footsteps sounded in the building, and a moment later Deputy Dewey appeared at his door.

Luke glanced up from his desk, hoping his deputy had some good news. "What's going on?"

Dewey glanced back at Harper's sleeping figure and lowered his voice, "We found some tracks in the woods."

"And?"

"They ended at a pier. I think this guy may have jumped into a boat and taken off."

Luke had considered that possibility before. It would explain why they'd lost his trail in the past. "Did you question anyone?"

"Everyone in the cabin next door was in town

partying. The other cabins weren't rented. In other words, no one saw anything."

Luke shifted his thoughts. Maybe he needed to tap into his deputies' knowledge of the town more. Cruise had lived here forever. And Dewey was quickly becoming a fixture around here.

Luke knew Dewey hung with a different, younger circle here in Fog Lake. Maybe he had a different perspective on Luke's theory.

"How long have you lived here, Dewey?" Luke asked.

"Two years. Came down from Kentucky. Why?"

He told him Harper's theory about a local being responsible.

Dewey blanched. "You really think one of our own could be behind this?"

Luke shrugged. He didn't want to believe it either, but he had to face the facts. "It makes sense. How else has this guy been disguising himself? He's been here six months now, at least."

"So what do you want me to do?" Dewey narrowed his eyes as he waited for Luke to respond.

"I just need you to give the theory some thought. I'm trying to remember who might have left here for several years only to return."

"And whoever that might be—whoever fits the description—is an automatic suspect?"

"I didn't say that. I'm just trying to formulate a list. I'm sure almost everyone on it will be cleared."

"Except for the killer."

Luke wished it was that easy. "This guy is smart. I'm sure he's covered his tracks. But I think this is worth exploring."

"Yes, sir, Sheriff. I'll see what I can find out."

"Thank you."

Dewey nodded toward Harper. "How is she doing?"

"She's shaken."

"It's a miracle she's alive."

Luke glanced at her sleeping figure, marveling at how peaceful she looked. "Yeah, it really is. She's a fast thinker. She got into that vent just in time. If she hadn't . . ."

"She might not be here with us right now."

"Exactly."

Dewey drew in a deep breath. "I'm going to get busy."

Harper's eyes flung open as an internal sense of urgency told her to wake up.

Darkness surrounded her—the darkness of night-time and slumber and . . . danger.

What had woken her?

Her eyes drifted to the distance, and she sucked in a breath.

Billy.

It was Billy.

He was here.

And he looked like the old Billy Harper she had known—with his Roman nose and thick hair and scrawny build. What had Shari been talking about? He hadn't had plastic surgery.

He stood over her bed with that detached look in his eyes.

Harper shot up and pulled the blanket closer around her, wishing it could protect her.

It couldn't.

Nothing could.

"What are you doing?" Her voice came out as a rasp.

"I'm watching."

"Why are you watching me?"

"You're pretty when you sleep."

"Billy, you need to leave. I don't want you watching me."

"Who said I was going to give you a choice?" A smile curled his lip.

Raw fear coursed through Harper. This guy had no conscience, did he? All he cared about was himself . . . and that made him dangerous. Terrifyingly dangerous.

"Get out of here."

"I don't want to."

"I said get out, Billy."

"But I'm imagining what it would be like to feel your blood between my fingers. It would be warm, especially at the beginning. And the smell of it . . . it would be like the first time I ever went hunting with my dad."

Her fear mingled with nausea.

He wanted to kill her.

And, if he did, he was going to enjoy it.

Focus, Harper. Focus. Don't let fear control you.

"You remember," she whispered, realizing what he'd just said.

Harper's father had never taken him hunting. All of this talk about his childhood memories being gone . . . it wasn't true, was it?

But why? What sense would it make?

"You went hunting with your father." Harper chose her words carefully in an effort to find out more information.

Billy said nothing.

"Why are you acting like you have no recollection?" she continued.

"It's not important."

"What is important?"

"I'm going to kill you, Harper."

Her heart pounded so hard in her ears that she could hardly hear anything else. Should she scream? She couldn't seem to do it. Find a weapon? All she had was her alarm clock beside her and a small lamp.

That was when she saw the knife gleaming in his hands.

Oh, dear Lord.

He leaned closer, and Harper froze, unable to do anything.

"But I'm not going to do it right now," he whispered. "It's not the right time."

"Why would you do this? What's wrong with you, Billy?"

"My dad . . . he saw this in me. He thought if he taught me to hunt that I might focus my energy on that sport. But it didn't work. In fact, it only fueled my desire to inflict pain. He couldn't handle it, so he abandoned me."

"I'm not a deer."

"You're my deer."

As he sliced the blade across her neck, she screamed.

And screamed.

And she couldn't stop.

"Harper! Harper! Wake up!"

She sat up straight and reached for her neck, expecting to feel blood there. She couldn't breathe, yet she gulped in air. Her heart pounded so badly that she thought she might pass out.

But wait. She wasn't at home.

She was . . .

Luke came into focus. He sat beside her. His hands were on her arms, holding her up, and his eyes wrinkled with concern.

"It was just a bad dream," he said. "You're safe."

Safe? Was she safe?

Harper felt like she'd turned into a puddle at his words.

That was right. She was at the sheriff's office.

Billy wasn't here.

Luke's arm went around her before she collapsed onto the floor. Harper was grateful he was there to hold her up. She wasn't sure she had the strength to support herself right now.

"I had a dream . . ." Or was it a dream? Could it be a flashback?

She didn't know.

"About Billy?" Luke asked.

She nodded and covered her face with her hands, trying to compose herself. "It was so real, Luke."

"What happened?"

"He was back in my bedroom. I was nineteen again. But . . ." Harper raised her head, which was now pounding. Reality and dreams mixed together. Which was real? She didn't know.

"But what, Harper?"

"In my dream, he told me that he went hunting with his father. He said his father noticed something evil in him. That's why he was abandoned on the streets. His father was scared of him."

Luke's eyes narrowed in thought. "Do you think that really happened? That he told you that?"

Her gaze met his. "I have no idea, Luke. I have no idea if that was a repressed memory or if it was just a crazy dream."

Chapter Twenty-One

HARPER SPLASHED water over her face in the small bathroom down the hallway at the sheriff's office.

Trembles still claimed her limbs as she cupped some water in her hands. The liquid barely reached her face, instead sloshing over the edges of her fingers.

That dream had felt so real. Too real.

And the terror that she'd felt? There was nothing fake about that.

She splashed more water in her face, trying to draw her thoughts away from the adrenaline-laced memories.

Billy was going to kill her, wasn't he?

A soft cry escaped, and Harper placed her hand over her lips, trying to silence any telltale sounds.

Billy had wanted to kill her seven years ago. And now Harper had come into town and walked into his web, practically begging him to finish what he started.

Her gut told her she was dealing with a true psycho here. There would be no reasoning with Billy. No compromise.

If he wanted Harper dead, the only thing that would end this was death itself—either his own death or hers.

She patted her face dry with some stiff paper towels from the metal dispenser beside her, tossed them into the trash, and then leaned her palms against the porcelain basin. As Harper stared at the reflection in the grainy mirror, she sighed.

She looked like she hadn't slept in days. Her hair looked limp in places and frizzy in other places. Circles hung beneath her eyes. Even her skin somehow seemed sallow.

Harper pulled her hair back into another sloppy bun. A few curly tendrils escaped and framed her face. Her friends worked for hours to make their hair look so naturally effortless.

This look would never fly in DC. Harper would be laughed out of the office if she came in wearing flannel, jeans, and no makeup. Thankfully, she wasn't in DC anymore. She'd never really liked dressing up anyway.

As Harper collected herself before stepping out, she glanced at her watch. It was seven a.m., and she desperately needed a bite to eat. And some coffee. She would guess that Luke did also.

She paused as she stepped into the lobby and

spotted Luke at his desk. He bent over it, studying some papers.

The man was a sight to behold. Even without sleep, he was handsome, more like a sheriff in one of those made-for-TV movies than someone Harper would expect to encounter in real life.

He hadn't shaved, and the shadow of a beard darkened his cheeks and chin. His dark, thick hair still looked surprisingly neat and in place.

As Luke glanced up and caught her staring, she looked away, gathering herself before plastering on a smile. She stepped toward the office, a sense of dread washing over her.

Was she imagining the connection between them? Was it their heightened emotions that caused her to feel this way? Or maybe the extraordinary events happening around them propelled them together?

She didn't know. She'd be lying if she said she didn't feel something between them.

However, the timing was awful. In fact, it couldn't be worse. Yet a small part of her felt like Luke was the silver lining in this whole experience.

She cleared her throat. "I'm going to get breakfast. What can I get you?"

"You don't have to get me anything."

"I insist. I'm just going to the diner. I could use a bite to eat."

"You can surprise me then. I'm not picky."

Harper doubted that. Luke seemed like the type

who knew exactly what he wanted. Despite that, she said, "Sure thing."

Luke stood, his chair rolling behind him, before Harper could step away. "Are you sure you're okay going to the diner alone?"

She nodded, shoving aside the memories of the haunting nightmare that wanted to come alive and control her. Harper wouldn't let it. "I'll be fine. It's daytime. I won't go anywhere else alone."

He seemed to hesitate before nodding. "Okay, then. Thank you."

But Harper couldn't deny that she felt a rush of fear as she left behind the security of the sheriff's office.

The brisk mountain air felt invigorating to Harper as she stepped outside. The autumn sunlight seemed to have burned away most of the fog—for now, at least. The streets were already filled with people—and there didn't appear to be any reporters on the prowl for a good story.

Part of Harper wanted to scream that everyone should leave.

The other part of her applauded people for not being bullied.

She paused on the corner. A man across the street caught her eye.

Danny Axton.

He stood in front of a coffeeshop, a cup in his hand. He talked to two people—maybe people who were helping him plan the festival. But his gaze was on Harper.

She shivered.

Why was that?

Did he recognize her? Could he be Billy?

Even though she'd seen the intruder in her cabin last night, she hadn't been able to make out details. Sure, he'd seemed huge in the shadows. But Harper's mind, in that moment, wasn't reliable. Fear had made everything bigger, more intense.

She pulled her gaze away and hurried across the street. As she stepped into the diner, her mind went back to her first night here.

To Shirley Cue.

She scolded herself for falling for the woman's story. Harper was usually much more of a skeptic than that. But she'd met a lot of people with crazy stories and names and personalities. In one way, being a reporter had made her think that she'd seen everything and heard everything. Little did she know how that would work to her detriment.

She glanced around now and saw the place was only half full, if that. The same oldies music—this time "Going to the Chapel"—played overhead, and the strangely comforting scent of bacon filled the air.

She went to the bar and grabbed a menu. She was going to guess that Luke was a meat-and-potatoes kind of breakfast guy. He'd certainly burn off all those calories over the next few days as he monitored the town.

She placed a to-go order for two all-American breakfast meals with the server behind the counter and then waited.

As she did, her phone rang. It was Ann. Perfect.

"Hey, girl," Harper answered. "Thanks for calling me back. I thought I was never going to get up with you."

"I've been out of the country for the past two weeks covering a story on the earthquake down in South America. My cell phone coverage was terrible."

"I'm impressed. You're in South America, yet you still managed to send me those articles."

Ann paused. "Those articles?"

"The ones on the murders in Fog Lake."

"Harper, you're losing me here. Say that again."

An icy feeling began to grow in Harper's gut. "Ann, the killings that match Billy's MO. You stumbled across them and sent them to me."

"What are you talking about?"

"You emailed me the information on the murders. It's your email address and everything." Harper knew something was wrong, but she wasn't ready to acknowledge it yet.

"What email?"

Harper put her friend on hold and scrolled back through her messages. Then she recited the email to her friend.

"Someone must have spoofed my email and added

that twenty-two after my name," Ann said. "It's close to my address, but it's not mine."

Harper thanked her friend and ended the call. But the chill in her gut turned into an all-out cold freeze. Someone had wanted her to come to this town.

And no one else made sense except Billy.

A cup of coffee appeared in front of Harper as she stood at the bar waiting for her food.

"You look like you could use this," a cheerful voice said.

Harper looked up at the server and smiled half-heartedly. "I look that bad, huh?"

He winked. "Just a little."

She'd seen this guy working here the night she'd come in. His age was hard to guess. He could be in his twenties or maybe even older. His receding hairline aged him, but his bright smile made him seem younger. He had pale skin, a thin build, and an easy-to-listen-to voice.

Harper glanced around. The diner wasn't that busy right now. Maybe she could talk to this guy. He would certainly have a good feel for what was going on here in town, and he seemed willing to chat.

"Could I ask you a question?" Harper started, taking a sip of her coffee.

"I only charge ten cents per answer. I'll add it to

your bill." He winked again, refilling someone else's coffee as his attention stayed on her.

Harper smiled, appreciating his lightheartedness. "I was in here two nights ago."

"Were you?"

"I guess you don't remember me?"

"You have an awfully big head, don't you?"

She squirmed, realizing she should have rephrased. "It's not that—"

"I'm just messing with you. Yes, I do remember." He flashed a grin.

Harper let out a laugh that sounded half-relieved and half-irritated. "I was sitting beside another woman. Do you remember that?"

"Vaguely. Why?" He pressed his hands on the counter, giving her his full attention.

"Did you recognize the other woman?"

He shrugged, scratching his neck. "No, should I? I figured the two of you were here together. Out of town. Visiting for the festival. On a girlfriend's weekend."

"No, I just met her when I came in. She said she was local."

"Well, if she's local, I've never seen her before. And I'm a local."

Another customer motioned him over, giving Harper the chance to study the server for a moment. Studied his average height. Dark hair.

Billy?

She just didn't know. And that she was even

considering it seemed crazy. She'd talked to Billy face-to-face when he was younger. She should recognize him if she ran into him.

But if what Shari had said was true, then maybe Billy was truly unrecognizable. With some weight-lifting, plastic surgery, colored contact lenses . . . people could transform themselves into someone completely new.

Was that what had happened?

He made his way back toward her, still seeming chatty and in good spirits.

"How long have you lived here?" Harper was careful to keep the accusatory tone from her voice. Nothing turned a person off from conversation more easily than that.

"Most of my life. I was born here, but my dad got transferred out to Nashville for his job. He worked for the railroad."

She sucked in a quick breath, trying not to jump to conclusions. "When did you come back?"

"I was about sixteen. My dad decided his job wasn't worth it. He came here and began working as a boat captain. It was a pay cut, but he's a whole lot happier. I bought this place last year, after saving up money working for my dad—plus some loans, of course."

His story sounded nice, like the all-American dream of doing what you loved. But people didn't always tell the truth. And Harper was hesitant to believe anyone. No, she had no idea whom to trust at this point, not since the killer's face was unknown. Not when he could pose as a friend.

But she added one more person to her suspect list. The diner owner.

She glanced at the tag on his shirt. Kyle Bennett.

She needed to keep him in mind.

Chapter Twenty-Two

WHAT IF THE killer's family still lived in town?

Luke chewed on the question. If Harper's dream was more than a dream—if it was a memory—then this guy's father had kicked him out. Maybe, just maybe, they could track him down through that tidbit.

He sighed and leaned back in the chair at his desk. He'd already had a busy morning.

He'd sent Dewey to question Ian.

He'd sent Cruise to pick up Harper's car for her. Luke had it towed to a local shop last night and had the tire repaired.

He'd called Harper's mom, Candance, curious about her last conversation with Billy. She'd hung up on him.

Luke had also perused all the news articles that had been published this morning on the murders here. He'd found eight that mentioned The Watcher and the town of Fog Lake.

With each new discovery, the tension in his gut grew.

He closed his eyes a moment and remembered the terror on Harper's face this morning. Her dream had obviously seemed real. Too real.

But what if it was more than that? What if it was some kind of repressed memory?

If that was the case then Luke needed to seriously consider the idea that this killer had grown up here in Fog Lake. Moved away. That his father, at least, had lived here. Had taught him to hunt. Had abandoned him.

Who in this town fit that profile? He needed to mull that over.

If Billy was alive and he came back into town, his father wouldn't greet him with open arms.

What if he'd killed his father?

Who had died here in town over the past six or seven months?

It was worth looking into.

Just then, his phone rang. It was the medical examiner out of Lynchburg. "I got your phone call, and I looked into the case. The only person we have on record dying in a car crash on that date was a man named Billy Jennings."

"How did you ascertain he was the one in the vehicle?" Luke asked.

"The car was registered to him. His driver's

license was intact, and confirmed his ID. We also did our basic examination. He fit the profile, and no one else was reported missing."

"So you didn't do an extensive examination?"

"There was no need to. Mr. Jennings' landlord confirmed he'd left home that morning to go to work for a construction company. We even found the ring Mr. Jennings always wore."

"How did the accident happen?"

Papers flipped in the background. "We're not sure what happened, but the basic conclusion was that he'd fallen asleep behind the wheel. The man he was renting a room from said he wasn't sleeping much. He'd been working two jobs."

"Two jobs?"

"That's correct. He only worked in this area on weekends. Otherwise, he traveled to Raleigh for work. Anyway, he went off the side of the road and hit a tree. The whole car caught on fire."

"I see. Thank you for calling me back. Could I get the name of his landlord?"

"Well, I can give it to you, but he died a month later."

Luke's back straightened. "How?"

"He got his prescription medications mixed up, and the result was fatal."

Just like Tom Brock, Luke realized.

Luke pondered his call with the ME. He was going to have to jump through some hoops in order to have the body exhumed and confirm who had actually died. But Luke was becoming more and more certain that Billy Jennings hadn't died in that accident.

No, he'd staged it.

He'd staged so much of this, hadn't he?

Nothing was confirmed yet, but Luke didn't like the picture that was coming together in his mind.

He stuck his head out the door, glancing at Ms. Mary who sat behind the front desk drinking her tea. "Ms. Mary, I need you to check the obituaries for me. I need the names of anyone from here who died six or seven months ago."

"Yes, sir. Anything in particular I need to look for?"

"It should be a man. Probably anywhere from his mid-forties into his sixties. The death could be by a natural cause or an accident." It wouldn't have obviously been a murder. No, there had been no homicides in this town for decades until now.

Everything had changed quickly.

"I'll get right on that," Ms. Mary said.

Deputy Dewey stepped into the station and sauntered toward him. "Harper's neighbor is out. He has an alibi for last night. Numerous people spotted him at Hanky's."

"At least, we can rule him out."

Dewey paused in the doorway. "Do you have another lead? I heard you asking about obituaries."

Luke shared his theory.

Dewey nodded slowly as he processed Luke's words. "It makes sense, I suppose. I have a new lead as well. I called the social worker from back in Raleigh, just like you asked, and I inquired about Billy. She finally called me back."

"What did she say?" Luke would take any new lead he could get right now.

"She clearly remembered Billy. Said he was charming. From the moment he was brought into the child protective services office, everyone fell in love with him."

"That's what Harper said—that he could be charming when he wanted to be. But that masked a deeper, darker side."

"She said the boy went through rounds and rounds of tests, and there was no indication he remembered anything about his past."

"What was her theory?"

"She figured his parents were poor, couldn't take care of him, and feared legal repercussions if they willingly gave him up. She thinks they left him on the streets instead with the hopes that someone would take him in."

"Good to know."

Dewey shifted. "She did say that when he first started talking—he was mute, initially—but that when he did begin speaking again, he had an accent."

"What kind?"

"A mountain accent."

Luke let that wash over him. "That would fit our theory."

Dewey offered a half-shrug and nodded, entirely too laid-back for his own good at times. "Yeah, that's what I thought too. What next?"

"We keep making that list of potential suspects here in town. We try to figure out how this guy is getting in and out of the houses without struggle."

"Will do."

Just then, Harper stepped back into the station with breakfast. And Luke had never seen a more welcome sight . . . but he wasn't sure if his realization had to do with seeing food or seeing Harper.

Harper closed her Styrofoam container, satisfied that she'd been able to eat some. Food could do a world of good. Luke seemed to share the sentiment. He looked like he'd enjoyed every bit of his breakfast as they'd sat in his office eating together.

As they'd eaten, she'd updated him on her conversation with Ann. Then she'd tried to give him some tips on dealing with the press, and he'd been surprisingly receptive.

She waited until after they finished to bring up Kyle Bennett, careful to add it was just a theory. The last thing she wanted was to implicate someone innocent.

Luke was going to have Deputy Cruise check the man's alibi for last night.

She rubbed her lips against each other as she considered the rest of her day. "I'd like to get cleaned up so I can feel human again and people will stop handing me free coffee."

Luke gave her a "huh?" expression.

"Never mind. But I thought I could find a hotel room—"

"Bad idea."

"How else am I going to get changed and cleaned up?"

He stared off in the distance for a moment before looking back at her. "I know this will sound strange, but how about if I take you to my place for now? My brother and sister are living there, so there won't be anything strange. I promise."

It was sweet of him to say that. Harper knew Luke was looking out for her, and that she was a target right now.

She chewed on the idea a moment.

"I need to get cleaned up myself." He paused. "I'd just feel better if you weren't alone right now. Getting breakfast is one thing. But going to a hotel alone . . . I doubt you can find anything available."

If Harper were honest, she'd admit she had no desire to go back to that cabin alone. But she was a single woman, and she had to do what she had to do. There was no backup plan.

But Luke's suggestion seemed to be a decent one. At least she'd have some sense of security. And she trusted Luke. She didn't know why. Maybe it was just a gut feeling. Either way, it didn't matter. He just might be the closest thing to a friend she had here in Fog Lake.

After a moment of thought, she nodded. "Okay then."

They left a few minutes later, picked up her things at the cabin, and then drove down the road in silence. Harper appreciated the quiet. Sometimes, the quiet could feel awkward. But not now. No, the quiet seemed comfortable and pleasant. It gave her time to sort through her thoughts.

Luke pulled to a stop in front of a log cabin that sat overlooking the lake.

Harper gazed up at the two-story house built onto the mountainside. Like so many homes in the area, it had an exposed basement. The property was well-kept with a man-made waterfall flowing into a little pond surrounded by smooth river rocks. A cozy wooden swing sat beside it, and the little bit of grass they had was cut short and neat.

"Nice," Harper muttered.

"This is where my dad grew up."

"You really do have roots in this area, don't you?"

Luke followed her gaze, staring at the house with a touch of wistfulness in his gaze. "Yeah, I do. My mom and dad were high school sweethearts. They never wanted to leave this place. My brother Boone moved in here after my dad died so he could help take care of our sister."

"Ansley?" Luke's family dynamic had Harper curious. Though Ansley had fiercely defended her brother during the confrontation in Hanky's, the two also appeared to be complete opposites.

Luke frowned, in no hurry to climb from his truck. "Yes, Ansley. She was only eighteen at the time. She was old enough to be on her own, but none of us thought that was a good idea."

"I see." Harper liked the idea of family looking out for each other. It beat the precedent her mom had set when she kicked Harper out.

"Then I moved back to Fog Lake, and it just made sense that I would live here also. There's plenty of space here at the house and more memories than I know what to do with."

Harper heard the grief in his words, and her heart leapt into her throat. It sounded like he'd been through a lot—too much, for that matter. "Well, thank you for letting me use it right now."

"Of course." Luke released his breath, seeming to expel the bad memories, and he opened his door. "Come on. We should get moving."

Luke's hand went to Harper's back as he led her inside. Just out of politeness, she reminded herself. He was being a gentleman. But the simple act somehow made her insides feel gooey.

And that was Harper's first sign that she was in trouble.

Chapter Twenty-Three

LUKE SUCKED in a breath when Harper stepped out of the hallway, her hair still wet. She offered a quick smile as she raked her hands through her damp curls. She'd changed into some new jeans and a yellow long-sleeved shirt.

She stepped closer and paused in front of him. "Thanks again for letting me use your place."

"No problem." His voice sounded thinner than he would like. He hadn't realized until now just how attracted he was to the woman. He usually wasn't this quick to feel things for someone. But there was something about Harper that was different.

He stepped back, thankful that he'd had the chance to freshen up himself. He'd showered, changed, and shaved. Just doing those things somehow made him feel more alert.

Harper glanced around the space—the dining

room beside the kitchen. Both rooms blended with the living area. "It's quiet around here. I was hoping I'd get to meet your brother. You said his name was Boone, right?"

"Yes. He's the middle brother. I also have a younger brother named Jaxon, who's in the military. He hasn't been home for six months because of deployment."

"I see. And then Ansley is the youngest?" Harper reached toward the table beside her and picked up one of the frames there.

"That's right." Luke glanced at the picture in Harper's hand. It was an old family photo, taken five years ago. Back when his mom was still here. When his dad was healthy. When Kathleen was still alive. When life didn't seem as hard.

Luke had come home from Atlanta for a week of vacation, and his mom had insisted on a new, updated family portrait. And it was a perfect picture with orange and yellow leaves smeared in the background. Faded blue mountains. Big, rocky boulders.

No one staring at that photo would guess that beneath the perfect family façade cancer lurked in his father's body. That his mom had been having an affair with Reggie Axton. That his sister would turn to drugs and alcohol. That Kathleen would die in a tragic accident.

What he wouldn't give sometimes to turn back time.

He cleared his throat. "Boone runs a tackle shop

and general store on the edge of town. Lots of campers give him his business there."

"An outdoorsman, huh?"

"Through and through. Nothing makes him happier than pitching a tent and casting a fishing line."

"It's good to find something that makes you happy."

Luke frowned and glanced at the happy family portrait once more, pointing to a woman there. "He needs a little bit of serenity. This was his wife Kathleen. She died five years ago while they were hiking on their honeymoon. Lots of people looked at him as a suspect. They didn't understand how an avid mountain climber like Kathleen could have slipped off a cliff and fallen to her death."

Harper's eyes widened as his words hit her. "That's horrible, Luke. Your family really has been through the valley, haven't they?"

"We really have. I like to think we can rebuild and come out stronger, but . . ."

Harper stepped closer and squeezed his arm. "There's always hope. It may not seem like it. But in those times when it seems impossible, we've got to hold onto that truth even more."

Luke smiled at her words. The woman had a lot of wisdom. He'd give her that.

She dropped her hand from his arm and licked her lips. Luke could sense a subject change.

"I know this is a strange question," Harper

started. "But I also know you're not going to let me out of your sight."

"What do you need, Harper?" In a different life, he could see himself bending over backward, eager to do anything that might bring a smile to this woman's face. Harper was the kind of girl a guy could give up everything for.

But this wasn't a different life. This was his real life, one with all of its challenges and too many responsibilities.

"I'd like to see the first two crime scenes," Harper said.

Luke tilted his head. "Why would you want to do that?"

She shrugged and glanced out the window before turning back to him. Her lips twisted together, as if she was struggling to describe her reasoning. "I can't explain it. I know it doesn't make much sense. But my dream last night . . . it triggered something in me. I can't help but wonder if answers might be closer than I think."

That dream really had shaken her up, hadn't it? He'd sensed a heavy spirit about her since she woke up. "And you think that seeing these crime scenes will spark some kind of memory?"

"I'm making no promises. But I know my mind won't be at rest until I see them for myself."

Luke considered everything he had to do. But maybe seeing those crime scenes would spark something new in him. Or, better yet, maybe they would spark a memory in Harper.

After all, she was the link here. Somehow, Harper was wrapped up in all of this.

The thought didn't settle well with him. "Okay, let's go then."

Harper glanced around the cabin where Victoria Ale had died. She knew only a little about the woman. Victoria was from Pittsburg. She'd come here to get away for a short vacation. She was twenty-nine and worked as a nurse at a children's hospital.

The place was a pretty standard rental. Log walls. Outdoorsy leather furniture. Big stone fireplace. Prints on the walls featuring bear, deer, and other wildlife.

"It's not rented," Harper said, pausing in the middle of the living room.

"It hasn't been rented since the murder. Somehow the address got out, and now no one wants to stay here."

Harper ran her hand along the kitchen counter. "I can understand that."

She paused and glanced at the floor by the entryway. If she closed her eyes, she could picture the body there. Picture the horror.

"That's where we found Victoria," Luke said, following her gaze.

"No evidence was left here either?"

He shook his head. "No, the scene was clean. No sign of forced entry. No sign of struggle. It doesn't make sense."

"Who can get into these buildings that easily?"

He shrugged. "A maintenance man, I suppose."

"Larry?"

"Yeah, Larry Wheeler. You know him?"

Harper shrugged, probably too quickly. "No, I don't know him. But I've seen him. Are these cabins all owned by the same people?"

"No, but they're managed by the same company. We looked into the employees, but we didn't find anything definitive."

"Have you talked to Larry?"

"Larry?" Luke repeated. "He wouldn't do this."

"How can you be sure? He's the right age. Right basic build. He has the connection."

"He was out of town when the first murder happened."

"You verified that?"

"Of course."

"Sorry. I'm not trying to question you. But it's just so weird that there's no evidence left behind."

"Danny Axton . . . his family owns the management company."

Harper's pulse spiked. "Did you look into him?"

Luke remained by the door, almost standing like a bodyguard there. "We've looked into everyone,

Harper. And no one stands out. Everyone in this town, in one way or another, seems to have motive, means, or opportunity. But no one has all three."

"What's Danny's alibi?"

"He was with his girlfriend."

"Does his girlfriend have straight hair and like to make up cutesy names for herself like Shirley Cue?"

"No, she doesn't. Although we did look into Shirley Cue. She was staying at one of the campgrounds. Of course, she used a fake name and address, and she disappeared shortly after we found Tom. The TBI is looking for her."

It was good to know that Luke had guys looking for the woman, at least. But Harper would guess the woman left town. She could be anywhere by now.

"What do you know about Danny's girlfriend?" Harper asked instead.

"Her name was Sabrina. They broke up." Luke paused, the edge of his lip pulling down in a frown. "I know you want to find something here, Harper, but we've already been through this place. There's nothing."

Her heart sagged, even though she realized the truth in his words. "I was hoping there would be something here, something . . . something intrinsic that I'd pick up on, I suppose. But you're right. I guess this was useless. I'm sorry. I know you had better things to do."

"It's okay. You ready to go?"

She nodded, disappointment biting more deeply than she'd thought it would. "Yeah, let's get out of here."

But, at the rate she was going, the killer would find her again well before she could ever hope to find him.

Chapter Twenty-Four

LUKE STEPPED from the cabin and glanced at the woods that bordered the place on one side. There, on a rocky incline, was a well-traveled path that his feet had graced on many occasions.

He was well aware of all the things he had to do. His workload was more than one person could manage right now, for that matter. But maybe clearing his head for a minute was the best thing he could do for this case.

He touched Harper's arm, stopping her before she went to his SUV. "Hey, one second."

Harper raised her eyebrows. "Yes?"

"This is going to seem strange, but I'd like to show you something. Just for a minute—well, maybe ten minutes. Are you up for a quick detour?"

"I'm intrigued."

Why was Luke doing this? He knew why. "Maybe

we both just need a quick mental break, you know? I have just the solution."

"Yeah, I do know all about needing mental breaks." Exhaustion tinged Harper's voice. "I'm game."

Luke helped Harper climb the initial entrance onto the trail—the steep incline was probably the hardest part of the hike. After that, the trail edged around the rim of the lake. Tall trees secluded any views, however.

For now.

Luke knew the trails in this area like the back of his hand. As a teen, all he'd wanted to do was explore the area and see what he could discover.

His dad had taught all the kids how to live off the land—to make fires, to use a compass, to fish. Luke's childhood was filled with so many simple memories, and, at times, he longed to go back to that period of his life.

The trees finally cleared, and Luke paused by a stone wall.

They gazed out at the overlook. The mountains rolled in blue, smoky peaks around them. Below them, the lake stretched as clear and smooth as a mirror this morning.

This was probably one of his favorite views of the lake.

"This is so beautiful," Harper muttered, staring over the landscape with a touch of awe in her voice.

"Isn't it? This is actually the area where explorer

Franklin Locke stood as he watched the massacre below."

Harper glanced up at him, a wrinkle between her brows. "The massacre?"

Luke nodded, surprised she hadn't heard about it yet. Then again, many people thought this was just local folklore. "Back in 1772. Locke wrote about it, even though his accounts never made many history books."

"You've got me hooked now. What happened?" Harper crossed her arms and turned toward him. "Someone started telling me this story earlier, and I've been curious about it ever since."

"Two rival Indian tribes—the Pogorip and the Bowakees—lived in this area."

"I've never even heard of them."

"Neither were well known, but the Pogorip lived around this lake. In fact, their name means fog."

"Interesting."

"Anyway, the two tribes had been in battle for years. And one day it all came to a head. They both met at the lake, ready to settle things once and for all." Luke glanced back at the lake, picturing it all play out, just as he'd done as a child when his father had told him these stories. "At least, that was the way it had always been. The leader of the Pogorip apparently got mad after his daughter married the son of the rival tribe. As they came for battle, his tribe launched into a surprise attack."

"Oh no."

"Right here on the shore of this lake, it's said that more than three hundred Indian warriors died. Neither of the tribes were ever the same. Eventually, they both died off. The few remaining members integrated into life with the settlers in the area."

Harper followed his gaze and stared out over the lake also. "It sounds like the area has had a tragic history for a long time."

"It does. On occasion, people will still find bones that date back hundreds of years—maybe from the massacre. Some people believe the spirits of those who died still haunt this area."

Harper's gaze flickered to his. "But you don't?"

He let out a soft laugh. "Oh, no. I don't. But I do feel like the area has some stains that we haven't been able to get rid of."

"Despite the tragedy of the past, I can see why you like it here."

He did like this area. Its beauty was unmatched. He supposed he just never saw this in his future, though. "When I was younger, I just wanted to leave. I didn't think this place had anything for me."

"You wanted to be a big city detective, didn't you?"

Luke could feel Harper studying him, trying to put the pieces of who he was together. It was a big task, one she'd most likely give up on soon when she discovered the pieces didn't easily fit.

"I did want to experience a different side of life than this small mountain town," Luke said. "But once

I got to the city, I never really liked it there. I never admitted that at the time, of course. But there was always a part of me that felt like I'd left a piece of me behind when I moved from Fog Lake."

"It's good when you can find a place like that. So many people feel like they never find a place to call home." Harper said the words with a certain wistfulness that showed she understood, that she felt like a woman without a real home.

The thought brought out a surge of protectiveness in him.

"I should have been here when my mom left. When my dad got sick. But I told myself that my job needed me." Luke's voice came out raspy as emotions tried to choke him.

Harper squeezed his arm and peered up at him with wide, compassionate eyes. "It's okay, Luke."

That was nice of her to say. But Luke knew it wasn't okay. He'd only come back here after his father had called and made him promise that he'd move home and take care of the family and town. His dad had been on his deathbed. How could Luke say no?

He couldn't.

And Luke liked to be a man of his word. So he had come back a week before his father passed.

He was glad he'd been able to be there during his father's last days. But he'd also realized that he should have been here way sooner. He hadn't fully realized the state his family had been in.

"Luke," Harper said softly, her voice tugging at him for attention.

He pulled his gaze away from one view and to another. Harper.

She looked gorgeous as she stood there with so much kindness and empathy in her gaze. With the mist softening the background behind her. With her curls springing to life, matching her tenacious spirit.

The woman had given up everything to come here and do what she believed was the right thing. She was facing her worst nightmare—possibly reliving the attack on her three years ago. An attack she would always wear a scar from.

She really was amazing.

"It's not your job to save everyone." Harper's tone sounded tender with concern.

"Sure it is. I'm the sheriff."

"Do what you can, but you put too much pressure on yourself. It's not healthy."

Luke let out a breath. Or was it a laugh? A skeptical laugh?

Harper's words were sweet. They really were. But Harper couldn't possibly understand all his responsibilities.

"It's not that easy, Harper." His voice was thick with emotion—emotion that he'd rather swallow. But it wasn't that simple, nor would it ever be. "It's just not that easy."

Harper didn't seem to buy what he'd told her. Fire lit in her eyes—fire mixed with what appeared to be determination and conviction. "Luke, I know you want to take care of your family and this town. But you take it beyond that. You feel guilt for things you have no control over. You've got to let that go. You're doing a good job, and you're doing all you can. No one can ask any more of you than that. And if they do? Then that's on them."

Her words washed over him, and the heaviness pressing on Luke almost felt like it lifted for a moment. Almost.

Luke's gaze shifted, and, as his eyes met Harper's, it felt like something cracked inside him. All the pressure he'd been feeling . . . the weight he'd been carrying . . . Harper could see it. Could understand it.

Harper was the first person since Luke had moved here to reassure him that he was . . . doing okay. That he didn't have to be everything to everybody. To acknowledge that he was trying his best to fight the good fight.

Luke didn't know what he was doing, but he stepped closer to Harper. One arm wrapped around her waist and the other skimmed her neck.

Her eyes widened at his nearness, but she didn't object or pull back.

Luke leaned closer. Close enough to smell the scent of honeysuckle and soap in Harper's hair. Close enough to hear her breathing in his ear. Close enough to feel a wave of electricity crackling between them.

Harper's hand fisted his jacket.

Her eyes closed.

Luke pulled her just an inch closer. That was all he needed.

His lips claimed hers.

Harper's arms wrapped around his neck, and her response made it clear that she felt the same connection he did.

Luke pulled away and caught his breath—though barely. His cheek was still nestled next to Harper's. He still stood close enough to feel her heart racing, the pulses easily matching his.

He didn't want to break the connection.

It had been a long, long time since he'd felt this way.

And the one person who'd brought out this side of him was a reporter.

If Luke didn't feel so content right now, he might laugh at the irony.

But reality lingered at the back of his mind—a reality he couldn't ignore, even as much as he might want to.

"Harper . . . I wasn't expecting this," he rasped, all too aware of her nearness.

"Me either." The emotion in her voice matched the emotion Luke felt.

"The timing . . ."

"Is awful," she finished. "I know. If we were a book, we could name it *Romance in the Time of Murder*."

As her words sank in, a deep chuckle emerged from his gut. The irony in this situation . . . it was either laugh at it or cry. He'd choose to laugh. Right now, at least. "You're funny."

"I wish I weren't."

His chuckle died, and he gazed at Harper again. He wished he could just enjoy her presence. That they could do things normal couples did—dinners, camp-fires, hikes. But that couldn't be a reality right now.

The burdens seemed to roll back onto his shoulders. They'd lifted—but only for a moment. And now that they were back, they felt heavier than ever.

"Harper, I've got to concentrate on this case right now. I can't . . . I can't get distracted by this." He desperately wished he could.

"No, you can't. I wouldn't expect you to."

Was this woman too good to be true? Because if Luke could put together his perfect woman, it would be Harper—if she wasn't a reporter. But she was understanding and kind and smart. And funny. Really funny sometimes.

He took a step back, drawing on every ounce of his self-control. "So we keep our distance until this is over."

Harper rubbed her lips together. "It's probably a good idea."

"Thank you."

She tilted her head. "For what?"

Luke didn't even know where to start. There was so much he could thank her for. Harper had been an answer to so many prayers. "Just thank you."

As Luke turned away from her, needing to put

some distance between himself and the temptation to pull Harper into his arms again, he heard a twig break in the woods behind them.

He turned just in time to see Danny Axton standing there.

Chapter Twenty-Five

HARPER GASPED when she spotted the man lurking between the trees. Staring. Watching.

Just like Billy used to watch her.

The man turned to flee, when Luke pulled out his gun and fired a warning shot.

"I've already seen you, Danny," Luke called. "Running won't do any good."

Danny froze. Lifted his hands. Turned with a look of defeat on his face.

"Come closer," Luke ordered.

Danny scowled, making it clear his obedience was begrudging, at best. But, despite that, he climbed from the woods until he stood in front of them.

Still holding his gun, Luke pushed Harper behind him. "What are you doing here?"

"I came to check on the cabin, and I saw you were here. I decided to check things out and see what you two were up to."

"You just happened to arrive at the same time? And you followed us through the woods?" Skepticism tinged Luke's voice.

Danny didn't flinch. "That's right. I don't trust no one anymore, including you."

"And why's that?"

"If the town fails, you'll be free to leave and do your own thing. I know you didn't want to come back here. This was your way out."

Luke scoffed. "You think I want the town of Fog Lake to die? How would that benefit me?"

Danny raised his chin, his eyes sparkling with defiance and . . . something else. "As a matter of fact, I do think that. This town, without its livelihood—tourism —would cease to exist. If it doesn't exist, it doesn't need a sheriff. You hate it here. You're only here out of obligation."

"That's not true." Luke's words came out a rumble.

The defiance in Danny's tone turned to satisfaction. "Your mom told me."

Harper glanced at Luke and saw his cheeks redden. "We're not going to talk about my mom right now."

The smug look remained on Danny's face. "Fine. What better way to shut down the town than by orchestrating a string of murders?"

Luke continued to bristle beside her. "I think you're off your rocker, Danny. I'm here to protect and serve the town, not to wreak havoc."

"Well, someone's responsible. Why haven't you found the person yet?" Danny's voice contained a mocking, arrogant tone that made Harper want to smack the man down to size.

"That's what I've been working on doing."

Harper moved from behind Luke, unable to keep her mouth shut any longer. "How do we know it's not you?"

It was Danny's turn to scoff. "Why would I do it?"

"You tell me. You're the one following us through the woods and trying to stir up trouble."

"I love this place. My heritage is here. My family history goes back to the Pogorips."

"That doesn't mean you're not guilty," Harper continued, feeling a surge of bravery—or was it stupidity?

"I have an alibi." Something gleamed in the man's eyes. "My girlfriend."

"Where's this girlfriend now?" Luke asked.

"I'll give you her number." Danny glowered at Harper. "Besides, maybe you're not innocent, either. I heard the town scuttlebutt. You think your brother is behind this. Maybe you're an accomplice."

Luke bristled beside her, but Harper put a hand on his arm to hold him back.

"My parents adopted him out of the foster system after I was out of the house," Harper said, careful to keep her emotion in check. "And I came here to help find him. So you can stop pointing that finger at me."

"That's just what you want, isn't it? But what I'm

wondering is this: What if you and your brother are working together? Because the only person in town that I've seen acting suspicious is you."

Harper sucked in a deep breath. Danny really thought she was a suspect? That's why he'd been giving her a strange look in town, wasn't it?

She glanced at Luke. What if he started believing that also? Because soon, the people in this town might be desperate enough for a witch hunt.

And Harper had made herself an easy target.

Luke was called down to the docks after someone's boat had been damaged by another boater. Harper could tell he was hesitant to leave her, but she promised to stay in the heart of the town, around people.

That seemed to appease him.

But something about Danny's words had caused a new wave of awareness for her. Were all the people who glanced her way wondering if she was affiliated with a killer? Or were they the innocent glances of people curious about the town?

Harper's objectivity was gone, leaving her with no idea.

Luke had told her to ignore Danny, insisting that he was just an overgrown bully. But his words were hard to forget.

She stood on the sidewalk a moment, right there

on Main Street, trying to collect her thoughts and figure out a plan of action.

Harper could sense the danger around her growing. This guy—most likely Billy—would strike again. He'd probably strike and try to finish what he'd started with Harper. But he could also veer off plan. This was no time to make guesses or take anything for granted.

He was hungry for another kill, and he wasn't going to stop until he got what he wanted.

Around Harper, the town was getting set up for the festival. More pumpkins and haybales were being brought out, along with scarecrows and an outhouse prop and plenty of photo opportunities. In the town square, there would be a hog roast and, for ten dollars, people could get a whole meal complete with barbecue, coleslaw, and beans.

But there was definitely a sense of hesitancy in the air. People who were here wanted to be here. But they were still nervous.

"Hey, Harper. Is that you?"

She turned around, anxious to see who'd called her—especially since she knew so few people here.

To her surprise, she saw Bryant Carmichael standing there. He was a reporter from a rival newspaper up in the capital—the *DC Ledger*. He looked very DC as he stood there in his expensive khakis and polo. The Asian man was trim, smart, and one of the most driven people Harper had ever met.

"Bryant, what are you doing here?"

"I'm covering the murders in town. You too? I thought you did politics."

"I'm actually here on a personal matter."

"Well, good timing. This story, when it breaks, is going to be big."

"Yes, it will be. Are you just waiting here for another murder to happen?" The words caused acid to rise in Harper's throat. It sounded so heartless. But Harper knew how journalism worked at times.

"Well, the town's sheriff certainly isn't being very open with details, so we're trying to track down our own."

"How's that going?"

"Locals are talkative. But you know how it is. We have to verify a lot of what we've heard."

"What theories are those?"

"Some people think an Indian warrior has come back to life and is exacting revenge."

She grunted. "It would make a good ghost story."

"I agree. Other people think someone hiding out in the mountains comes out of his isolation for long enough to do the deed."

"Another interesting theory. What do you think?"

"I think . . . I have no idea. But I feel sorry for this town."

"Why's that?"

"Because I don't see how it's going to survive this."

Just as he said the words, Harper glanced up. A chill washed over her.

Someone was watching her, she realized.

She scanned the crowd until her gaze stopped on one person.

The maintenance man. Larry.

He stood across the street, a trash bag in hand. But he was staring at Harper without apology.

Luke sat at his desk, trying to deny the fact that he was exhausted and invigorated at the same time. The paradox only made his head spin, yet the balance gave him just enough strength to go on.

He'd called in the state police, and they should be arriving within the next few hours. Whenever the town had their big festivals, he had to call in additional help. There just weren't enough people on his staff to do all the heavy lifting, especially since these festivals seemed to always bring out the troublemakers.

And now with The Watcher on the loose, things were even uglier.

He hoped he wasn't making a huge mistake by allowing this festival to go on. If anyone else died because of his decisions . . . he didn't know how he would live with himself.

Especially if that person was Harper.

He hadn't expected his feelings for her to grow so rapidly. But they had.

The woman had a fire inside her that he found refreshing.

Because his mom had left the family, he'd always proceeded with relationships very carefully. He didn't want to go through a loss like that again. And if a mom would leave her children and dying husband . . . it didn't leave him much hope for trusting anyone else.

But something about Harper was different.

She sacrificed whatever was needed in order to do the right thing. That showed a lot of determination and principle.

Luke took another sip of his now-cold coffee and turned back to the files on his desk. He had to concentrate on this case.

Ms. Mary had gotten back with him, giving him a list of everyone who'd died for any reason in this town over the past six months. He scanned the list. Other than the murder victims, there were seven names. Most had been older, elderly, for that matter. One man had died in an auto accident.

He was going to send his deputies to talk to the families of three people on the list.

He didn't have much hope that this lead would go anywhere—not now that he'd seen the names. But he wanted to follow through, just in case.

Ms. Mary was still working on putting together a list of any locals who'd moved out of town as a child only to move back later.

Right now, Cruise and Dewey were out setting up signs to help direct traffic tomorrow. It seemed so inconsequential to do that with everything that was going on.

But life continued, and, since that was the case, the ordinary had to take place despite the extraordinary.

Luke opened the file folder with all the information on this case.

He studied it every day, hoping to find a new clue. For something new to hit him or make him see evidence in a new light.

And he would do the same today.

He examined the crime-scene photos. Most were gruesome and still made his stomach turn, despite his years in law enforcement.

Then he flipped through the other photos of the cabins. Each cabin looked pretty typical, though they were managed by the same company. There were only two management companies in the area, so that wasn't surprising.

He paused at a photo of the bookshelf and studied it closer.

One of the framed photos on the shelf seemed familiar. Where had he seen it before?

It was a picture of an old cabin with a tin roof nestled in the mountains.

Out of curiosity, Luke flipped through pictures from the second crime scene.

His heart rate sped.

Wait . . . a picture of the same cabin was there.

Coincidence?

Maybe.

But maybe not.

He checked the house where the first murder had taken place. The same photo. Finally, he checked the photos from the Whistling Pines cabin where Harper had been staying.

Bingo!

It was there also.

Had the killer left this clue?

Why hadn't they seen it before?

Chapter Twenty-Six

LUKE HEARD the door to the station jangle and looked up to see Dewey walk in.

Perfect. He needed another set of eyes right now.

"Dewey!" Luke called. "Come in here."

The deputy sauntered into his office. "Yes, Sheriff."

Luke had enlarged the crime-scene photo on his computer so he could see the picture of the cabin more clearly. He angled the computer screen toward Dewey. "You recognize this place? The cabin?"

Luke had tried and tried to think about if he'd seen the place before, but he'd come up blank. There were so many cabins in the area.

"Hmm." Dewey squinted at the computer. "It's hard to say, but . . . that metal windmill in the flowerbed looks familiar."

"That's what I thought too, but I can't place it."

"You know, it almost looks like Kyle Bennett's place."

Luke's heart jumped a beat. Kyle Bennett? The man had just come to the area around five years ago. He fit the age profile of the killer. Could Kyle be their guy? Harper had mentioned him also.

"What's going on, Sheriff?" Dewey turned toward him with inquisitive eyes.

Luke stood and grabbed his hat. "We need to go pay Kyle a visit. I'll fill you in on the way there."

Luke turned on his lights as they traveled up the mountain to the remote location where Kyle's cabin was. Luke had never been here before, but he had passed it on his way to go rock climbing with his brother once.

The area was secluded, one of the homes that was up higher on the hillside than most. Luke knew a little about Kyle. The man was probably five years younger than he was, so they hadn't been in school together. He vaguely remembered Kyle growing up with a single dad and a brother.

As he drove, Dewey called the management company. Luke had sent over the photo earlier, but he needed a faster response. Hopefully, the woman on the phone would have an answer for him.

Dewey hung up. "They don't recognize the picture."

That was what Luke had figured.

"What do you know about Kyle?" Luke asked.

Dewey would be closer to his age—maybe they had been classmates or played on sports teams together.

Dewey shrugged. "I don't know him well. His food at the diner is decent. He . . ."

"What?" Luke had heard the start of something deeper in Dewey's voice.

"I'm assuming he's a suspect, that he could be The Watcher, and that's what this is about. Kyle's great grandparents, if I remember correctly, were Native American. Some people forget their heritage, but a lot of those Native American traditions carried over into his family life."

"Like the instruments, maybe?" Kyle seemed more and more like the right guy. His cabin. His history. His timeline in the town.

Luke pulled up to Kyle's place and threw the SUV in Park. He observed the building a moment.

This was definitely the place from the photo, all the way down to the metal windmill in the flowerbed.

But now that he could see it up close, he spotted the Indian dream catchers in the windows. A feather hanging near the door. Some crude weapons—like a blow gun and bow and arrow—by the side of the house.

With a nod toward Dewey, he walked up the front steps of the cabin. When he was sure Dewey was behind him as backup, Luke knocked. A chorus of dogs began barking on the other side of the door.

"Sheriff's Department," Luke called. "Open up."

A moment later, the door cracked. A man stood

there, staring at them.

Elmer, Luke remembered. Kyle's younger brother.

The man had always been eccentric and more of a homebody. And he made some Native American arts and crafts—like those dream catchers—and sold them at some local gift stores.

He had dark hair that he wore long, a broad nose, and a face that seemed incapable of smiling.

"What do you want?" Elmer grumbled.

His dogs continued to bark through the crack at the door. There had to be at least three of them. And the canines were large. Pit bulls? Maybe.

"I need to look inside your place," Luke told him, raising his voice to be heard over the dogs.

Elmer's eyes narrowed with suspicion. "Why would I let you do that?"

"Because we're investigating a murder," Luke stated, not mincing words.

Elmer blinked, as if unaffected by his statement. "I have nothing to do with any murders."

"It's not you we're investigating." Luke kept his tone nonconfrontational, even though his agitation grew at every bark he heard.

Elmer's gaze seemed to relax before instantly igniting again. "My brother? Kyle? He would never do something like that."

"Then you won't mind if we search your place?"

The door opened farther. "Be my guest. But you'll have to deal with my dogs."

Luke stepped inside. He'd never minded dogs

before—but he had to be careful.

He held out his hand, and the dogs sniffed. After a moment, they calmed down and Luke motioned for Dewey to come inside and begin searching.

Luke stayed close to Elmer. "So you're Kyle's younger brother?"

"That's right. I work from home making some dream catchers and trying to keep my family's heritage alive. My goal is to one day open a cultural center, much like what they've done down in Cherokee."

"Sounds noble. You guys just moved back here four or five years ago, correct?" Luke remained on his guard, his hand ready to grab his gun if necessary.

He didn't think it would be. The dogs had calmed down, and Elmer seemed calm—almost too stoic. Between the stench of the dogs, Luke detected an earthy scent. Marijuana.

That would explain Elmer's relaxed state.

"That's right," Elmer said. "But we grew up here. Dad's job took us to Nashville. Why you asking? This doesn't have to do with that serial killer, does it? The Watcher?"

Luke's jaw flexed. "I can't answer that question."

"Kyle would never hurt no one."

"Sheriff, come see this," Dewey called from down the hallway, most likely where the bedrooms were located.

Luke crossed the creaky wooden floor and stepped inside the first door. A bedroom, just as he suspected.

And a messy one at that. Based on the nametag he spotted on the dresser, he'd guess this was Kyle's room.

Dewey used a glove to hold something up.

A knife.

On the tip of it, there was dried blood.

———

Harper sat on a bench facing Fog Lake, trying to sort out her thoughts.

Her thoughts about Kyle Bennett.

About the fact that she'd been lured to this town.

About the fact that she could have easily been killed last night.

Maybe Luke was finding more answers than questions. Harper wanted to stop by the station and find out, but she didn't. Not yet.

He needed his space to work, and Harper didn't plan on hovering over him.

Yet a restlessness stirred inside her. She'd dropped everything. Come out here to Fog Lake. And she was no closer to the truth than she'd been before. No, the only thing she was closer to was death. Harper shivered at the thought.

Because she had a feeling Billy would try again. Would he be successful this time?

Her shiver deepened.

She decided to grab a cup of coffee and try to clear her head.

But just as she stepped toward the coffee shop, a face in the distance caught her eye.

It was Shirley Cue—or whatever her real name was.

The woman spotted Harper at the same time and took off in a run. Harper sprinted after her.

She easily caught up with the woman, who was five inches shorter and twenty pounds heavier. Harper grabbed her arm and twirled her around until their gazes met, and they faced off there on the sidewalk.

"Who are you?" Harper demanded.

The woman's eyes narrowed, almost as if she were annoyed. "It's not important."

"It's important to me. You almost got me killed." Harper's voice trembled under the weight of her emotions. This woman wasn't innocent. She'd been an accomplice to the crime. Had she helped to kill Tom Brock also?

The woman's gaze softened. "I didn't know that was going to happen until I heard murmurings about it here in town afterward."

"You need to start talking. I have the sheriff on speed dial, and I'm sure he'd love a face-to-face with you."

The woman tried to jerk away, but Harper didn't ease her grasp.

"Okay, okay. I'll talk." The woman suddenly didn't seem like the friendly, small-town girl who'd struck up a conversation at the diner. "It's like I said, I had no idea the way things would play out."

"Please explain. Because right now, you're looking like an accessory to a crime—a very serious crime."

The woman's face paled, and she blurted, "Someone paid me to have that conversation with you."

"Who?" Harper glowered down at her, appalled at the woman's words. Paid her? Even if that was true, it was still despicable.

"I don't know. I didn't see his face."

"You're going to have to give me more than that."

"It's like this. I came into town for the festival. I did know about the murders here, and, honestly, that made me want to come even more. I have an affinity for scary stuff. I was walking down by the lake when someone called me over. He was in a boathouse, and his face was shadowed. I couldn't see him."

Harper found that hard to believe. "You couldn't see anything?"

"No, I couldn't. I know how that sounds, but . . . I really have no idea how he looks."

"What did he say to you?"

Shirley's words came out fast, nervous. "He told me to find you—he described you very well—and to strike up a conversation. He said if you asked about what was going on in this town, I should direct you to visit the town historian at that address I gave you. That was it."

"That didn't sound suspicious to you?"

"No. It sounded like he wanted to relay information to you without being seen. I figured he was the town bad boy or that you two had some history. I never dreamed there would be a dead body there."

"How much did he give you?"

"A hundred dollars. It may not be much to some people, but I don't have a job. My dream is to be a vagabond. I needed the money. That guy must have been able to sense it."

"Why didn't you come forward with this information earlier? In fact, I'm surprised you even hung around town."

"I've been camping out in the middle of the woods, waiting for things to pass. I didn't want to miss out on the festival. It's my favorite."

"So you stayed in the area, even though you knew the police were looking for you?" Was this woman high? She very well might be. Either that or she had terrible judgment.

"Maybe. Lots of people wear costumes at the festival. I figured no one would be looking at me."

"You're going to have to share this with the sheriff," Harper told her. "He needs to know."

"I don't want to be arrested." The woman's voice pitched higher.

Good. Maybe she'd realized exactly what she'd done—the weight of her actions.

"Tell him what you told me, and maybe he'll be lenient. But hiding just makes you look guilty."

Before they could turn to walk down the street, someone ran past. It was a woman, and she sprinted toward a man who stood near a fountain. Her boyfriend, Harper would guess.

"Did you hear?" she said.

"Hear what?" The man stood and shoved his hands into his pocket.

"They just arrested The Watcher."

What? Harper needed to get to the sheriff's office. Now.

And she was bringing Shirley—or whatever her real name was—with her.

Luke stared at Kyle Bennett from across the table in the interrogation room.

"You're saying this isn't your knife," Luke held up the plastic evidence bag with the blood-tipped weapon inside.

"I've never seen it before."

Luke studied the man. Gone was the diner owner with a ready smile and easy jokes. Those traits had been replaced by panic—full-out panic. The kind that turned people's skin pale, that made their voice quiver, and that caused their eyes to widen and dart about in uncertainty.

"If you've never seen this knife before, then how did it get into your room?" Luke asked.

"I'm telling you—I have no idea." Kyle's voice broke, and he covered his eyes with his hands. "I didn't kill those women."

"We found the pictures also, Kyle."

In Kyle's drawers, beneath his clothing, they'd found photos of each of his victims. Each picture was more of a surveillance-style snapshot, taken when the women were unaware. Fingerprints had been found on the photos and were being run through the system now.

The evidence stacking up against Kyle was irrefutable. He even left the diner early last night because he had something he needed to do. He claimed he'd been illegally disposing of some cooking oil. Cruise was looking into that now.

Yet the man still denied being the murderer.

"I'm being set up," he said.

"Who would have set you up?" Luke had to admit —all of this surprised him.

Kyle had always seemed like a standup guy, and he'd never given Luke a bad gut feeling. Then again, the best criminals were subtle. Kyle, in his position at the diner, would have seen a lot of people who came through town. It would have been easy to pick out his victims.

He shrugged, his eyes wide and desperate. "I don't know. I have no idea. My brother, maybe?"

"Why would your brother do that?"

"Because he's weird."

"So you're implying your brother is the killer?"

Kyle seemed to realize what he'd said and blanched. "What? No! That's not what I meant."

"Then how else would he have gotten the

evidence?"

Kyle swung his head back and forth. "I have no idea. I just know that stuff isn't mine. I didn't put it there. And I don't know who did."

Luke leaned back. "If you didn't do this, then who would have had access to your cabin?"

Kyle shrugged. "Anyone. I mean, we don't lock our doors at night. We're out in the country. Our biggest worries are bears and the occasional coyote."

Things still didn't mesh in Luke's mind. "Why would someone set you up?"

"To take the blame off themselves. Why else?"

"Let's say that's true. Anyone have a vendetta against you? Because someone would really need to hate you to set you up like this."

Kyle looked off into the distance, offered a frustrated shrug, and then shook his head. "I don't know. I know I keep saying that, but I don't know. I guess the only person I've ever really had a beef with here in town is Danny Axton."

There was that name again. Interesting.

"What was that beef over?" Luke asked.

"The fact that the man is a jerk. Every time he comes into my diner, he complains about the food and wants to get it for free. I finally told him no. I don't care who his family is around here. He's not going to walk on me or get special privileges."

"Seems like a petty reason to set you up for murder, though."

"Well, that's all I've got. I don't know what else to

say." Kyle threw his hands in the air, almost like he was giving up and his soul had deflated right along with his last sentence.

"Did you rethink that lawyer yet?"

Kyle lowered his eyes with defeat. "No, but I guess I should."

Harper had left Shirley at the station with Deputy Cruise. Luke had been involved with something he couldn't be pulled away from. Instead, she was trying to trust that Deputy Cruise knew what he was doing.

Luke had left her a message with Ms. Mary at the front desk, asking Harper to meet him at his house for a late dinner. He said she could go over whenever she liked, and that he would be there as soon as he could.

Her car keys had also been waiting there.

Luke had her tire fixed.

That was entirely too sweet. He'd definitely gone above and beyond, a fact that she appreciated.

Knowing she could use a moment to catch her breath, Harper decided to take him up on his offer.

When she got to Luke's house, no one was there. Harper let herself in using a key Luke had given her and placed her bag in the spare bedroom, just as Luke had directed.

She'd only been there for ten minutes when the front door opened.

She desperately hoped it was Luke, and that he

had an update for her.

Instead. . . another man stepped inside.

A man who looked a lot like Luke.

A smile lit his face as he dropped his keys on a table by the entry. "You must be Harper. I'm Boone."

She patted her heart quickly, fussing at herself for overreacting. "Sorry, I'm a little jumpy. Yes, I'm Harper."

"I heard you might be here. Didn't mean to scare you. Luke said he's on his way. I'm going to start dinner." He held up something wrapped in newspaper in his hands.

"I can help."

"I never refuse help." He set the object on the kitchen counter and pulled off his jacket. "You like trout?"

"I can't say I've ever had it, but I'm totally down with trying something new."

Boone washed his hands before pulling out pots and pans and ingredients. A moment later, she began chopping up vegetables for a salad while Boone prepared the fish.

He was handsome, but in a more relaxed way than his older brother. Boone's hair was a little too long to be considered well-groomed—long enough that it curled at the ends. He had a shadow of a beard. Dancing eyes. A leaner build.

He definitely seemed like the more laid-back of the two, yet a heaviness lurked in the back of his gaze. She couldn't imagine what it would be like to lose a spouse on your honeymoon—and then for some people to suspect you of the crime.

"So you're a journalist, huh?" Boone started, pouring some oil into the pan.

"I am." She placed some shredded carrots on top of the pre-cut romaine lettuce.

"That's perfect." His tone sounded mildly amused.

"What do you mean?"

Boone glanced at her. "Luke didn't tell you?"

"I guess he didn't." Now she was curious.

"Luke was working a big case down in Atlanta—a serial killer. A reporter caught wind of it, found out some information and leaked it. The sting operation went south, and the killer shot a police officer. Luke hasn't liked reporters since then."

Was that why Luke had reacted so poorly when they'd first met and he learned Harper was a reporter? It would make sense. "I can understand why. But I'm not that kind of reporter."

"Obviously. You wouldn't be here if you were."

As Harper topped the salad with some tomatoes, she glanced back, taking a better look at Boone.

"Did you catch these fish?" Harper asked. The trout smelled surprisingly good, even though it wouldn't normally be her thing.

"I did. I like to fish on my days off—and that's what today is." He flipped one of the browned fillets over. "Anyway, I heard the town scuttlebutt."

She jerked her gaze toward him, uncertain if she'd

heard correctly. "That the killer had been captured?"

"Yep. I'm anxious to hear those words from Luke himself."

"Me too." Her heart pounded with a surprising anxiety. She should feel relieved. Yet she wouldn't feel better until she heard confirmation. That would explain why he was occupied at the station, however. "Did you hear who it was?"

"Rumor has it that it was Kyle Bennett."

Harper sucked in a quick breath. "Kyle Bennett? From the diner?"

"He's the one."

Harper blinked as she processed that. She'd considered whether or not Kyle was a suspect herself. But she could hardly wait to hear the details, to learn what had solidified him as the killer.

Could this nightmare really be over?

It looked like she wouldn't have to wait any longer for answers.

The door opened, and Luke stepped into the house.

Harper waited until Luke and Boone said hello to each other. Waited until Luke stripped off his jacket, hung it in the closet, and set his gun and radio on the table. Waited until he grabbed a bottle of water from the fridge and came to stand beside her and Boone.

"Is it true?" Harper finally asked, unable to hold

her question in any longer.

"We caught him," Luke said, satisfaction stretching across his voice. "The killer is in custody. He's finally in custody."

He uncapped the water and took a drink.

Harper let out a breath of relief—that ended up sounding more like a cry of joy.

"Kyle admitted to it?" Harper's heart surged with hope.

Luke's eyes lost a little of their glow. He took another long sip of water, signs of exhaustion showing on him. The past few days had been brutal on him.

"No, Kyle hasn't admitted to it. Not yet. But we have evidence that places Kyle at the crime scene. After we get that knife and blood tested, we should know something definitive. TBI is coming to help out more. They're taking Kyle into custody, and they'll test the knife."

"That's . . . great. How did you figure it out?"

"Don't let this information leave this room," Luke started. "But the killer had left behind a picture of a cabin at each of the crime scenes. It was left with the rest of the decorations, so it blended in. It's like he was teasing us. We found the cabin from the photo, and it belonged to Kyle Bennett. The knife was there, as well as pictures of the victims."

"That's fantastic," Boone said.

Luke nodded. "Yeah, maybe this town can finally relax, and the people here can have a real reason to celebrate."

Harper needed to know if he was Billy. She had so many questions. Why had he chosen to open a diner of all things? Why here in Fog Lake? "Could I talk to Kyle before TBI takes him away?"

Luke's smile disappeared as he shook his head. "Not yet. It's too soon. We need to wait for that evidence to come back first. I can't do anything to jeopardize the case, Harper. One wrong move, and Kyle could walk. I've seen it happen before. We can't risk it."

"I understand." But that didn't stop disappointment from squeezing at her gut. "I guess I can go back to the Whistling Pines tonight if they have a room."

His gaze captured hers, saying entirely more than words could. It said that he cared about her and wanted her close. "I'd still feel better if you stayed here."

"But you have the killer in custody." There should be no reason for her to be afraid . . . or unsafe.

"I know." Luke raised his hand as if trying to temper Harper's reaction. "My mind knows that. My adrenaline still tells me to be safe."

"We have plenty of room," Boone said, plating up the trout and pulling some potato salad from the fridge. "Besides, there are a lot of troublemakers around at this time of year. The festival brings them out. People who drink too much and start looking for reasons to get attention."

"Well, if you don't mind, then I will stay here."

The trout was surprisingly tasty, and listening to Boone talk about his adventures fishing, camping, mountain biking, and doing anything else outside was fascinating. A nice change of pace from talks of killers and crime. Yet Harper's mind couldn't get away from it.

When they finished dinner, it was already eight, and all she wanted to do was rest.

"Thank you for the meal," she started. "It was wonderful."

"Anytime," Boone said. "Listen, you look exhausted. I'll get this cleaned up if you want to rest."

"Are you sure?" Harper asked.

"Positive. It was nice to meet you, Harper."

She smiled and stood. "You too."

Luke followed her lead and crossed to her side of the table. "I'll walk you upstairs."

He placed a hand on her back and led Harper up the steps to a hallway with five doors running down the length of it.

He stopped outside her door and turned toward her.

"Thank you for everything," Harper started.

"It was no problem. All in a day's work."

"If this is in a day's work then every town should have a sheriff like you." She grinned.

"Well, I can't guarantee everyone would get such specialized attention."

"I should hope not." Her smile drifted as she remembered their promise to hold off on pursuing anything until this case was over. Kyle might be in custody, but this case still felt a long way from being done. "Goodnight, Luke."

"Goodnight."

She turned to step away when Luke called to her again with a soft, "Hey."

Harper paused.

He reached out his hand and, after a moment, Harper took it, uncertain where he was going with this. He drew her closer, his voice dropping lower as she felt his body heat next to hers.

"Goodnight," he murmured, studying her gaze with intensity. Sincerity. Warmth.

"I think you already said that."

But he didn't let go. Instead, he pulled Harper toward him and wrapped her in his warm embrace.

She briefly considered fighting it. But who was she kidding? She had no desire to at the moment. Instead she melted in his arms, resting for just a moment in the comfort of Luke's strength.

She didn't let go until Luke did—and even then it was just barely. His arms were still around her, just not as tight. Loose enough that she could pull back and see his face.

"What was that for?" Harper studied the lines and curves of his face, the glow of his eyes, and smoothness of his lips. She could gaze at his face all day and never get tired.

"Just because."

She cocked the side of her lip up in a teasing smile. "Is this how you say goodnight to all the potential murder targets in town?"

"Not quite." His voice contained a hint of amusement.

"Good. Just checking."

Luke grinned down at her, the action soft and warm. "I know I should let go."

Harper reached up and skimmed her fingers along the edge of his smooth jaw. "Maybe. But you know what?"

"What?"

She ran her finger over his cheek. "You have dimples when you smile."

"Do I?"

"And you know what's even more amazing? This is the first time I've noticed, which just might mean it's the first time you've actually smiled around me."

"I haven't had a reason to smile in a long time."

Their gazes caught, and that same unseen force seemed to sweep around them, creating some kind of capsule that trapped them, that made them forget everything else.

Luke's hand rested at her neck, and his eyes lit with warmth.

He wanted to kiss her again.

And Harper wasn't going to lie.

She wanted to kiss him too.

It would be so easy to do just that. To close her eyes. To move closer. To get lost in the moment.

"Um . . . sorry," someone said in the distance.

They both jumped away from each other.

Harper turned and saw Ansley standing at the top of the stairs, a mild look of amusement in her gaze.

"I didn't mean to interrupt." Her voice didn't sound all that apologetic.

Luke stepped back and shoved his hands into his pockets. "You weren't."

Ansley's look clearly stated she didn't believe him.

Harper thumped her hand over her shoulder. "I should go to bed."

Luke nodded, that lazy grin still on his face. "Goodnight."

"Goodnight."

Harper found herself humming as she got ready for bed. Which was crazy. There was so much going on. So much danger. So much to fear.

Yet, in the middle of the storm, she and Luke had sprung to life.

Someone knocked at her door. She turned, halfway expecting to see Luke there.

Instead, it was Ansley.

She stepped into the room before Harper could say anything and closed the door behind her. Harper studied her a moment. She looked different now than she did in the family portrait. No, in that picture she'd had dark curly hair—not as curly as Harper's but still curly. She'd had a bright smile and the "girl next door" look.

Now she looked gaunt. Her hair was short, straight, and blonde.

She hardly looked like the same person.

Harper instinctively knew this wasn't going to be an easy conversation. She knew how protective brothers and sisters could be of each other. She'd seen it firsthand at Hanky's that night.

"Hey, Ansley." Harper put down the bottle of lotion she'd been slathering on her face and pulled her legs beneath her as she sat on the bed.

"Hey, Harper." She stood off at a distance, an analytical look in her eyes. "So you and my brother, huh?"

Harper shrugged. "I'm just as surprised as anyone. But we're taking it slow, especially with the investigation right now."

"I haven't seen him look like that in a long time."

"Look like what?"

"Happy."

A warm burst filled Harper's chest—so warm it surprised even her. "Is that right?"

"He usually walks around acting like he has the weight of the world on his shoulders. And by world, I mean this town. This family. Me." Ansley frowned.

"He does have a lot of pressure on him right now, Ansley."

"He takes himself too seriously. I'm a big girl." Ansley seemed to sense the hidden message targeted at her.

"You might be. But when you drink too much, you lose all the wisdom of being a big girl." Maybe Harper shouldn't have said it. But how could she not?

Ansley's eyes narrowed. "Now you sound like my brother."

"Look, I know I'm overstepping here. But just hear me out for a minute. I can't imagine what you've been through. Your mom left. Your dad passed away. And I'm sure that left you feeling lost, probably angry. Confused."

"How would you know?" A defensive edge sharpened Ansley's voice. Gone was the overly confident woman from earlier, and in her place was a girl with no mother or father and a world of hurt.

Harper readjusted her legs so she could sit up straighter. "Because my mom kicked me out when I was nineteen. My dad didn't even come to my defense or act like he cared. Meanwhile, everyone was hailing her as Mom of the Year. Magazines wrote about her. No one knew the truth."

"What did you do?"

Harper seemed to have her attention, at least. "I had to make some serious choices. I was literally all alone. My mom had called my friends' parents and told them to keep their kids away from me. Told them I was trouble."

Ansley squinted. "What did you do to make her hate you so much?"

Ansley's words stung. But Harper had asked herself the same things so many times. What had she done?

The questions led Harper to the conclusion that this was her fault. That she'd done something wrong.

She supposed it was her fault that the reality show never happened. She'd called the producer herself and told him the truth about the family.

She hadn't wanted her brothers and sisters to be put through that. Being on TV . . . it would have catapulted her mother to instant fame and led her to be even more controlling and exacting.

It would have ruined everyone's lives.

"I stood up for what I thought was right, and it cost me everything," Harper said. "I spent the first night on the streets, and I met a crowd of people there who would have accepted me. They would accept anyone as long as they were willing to get high with them. And it was tempting. It was so tempting."

"And what did you do?"

Her mind drifted back to those days. "I got a job. I applied for loans. I went to college, and I paid my own way. And let me tell you—it was hard. It was a lot of work. But when I look in the mirror, I see someone I can live with. I'm not ashamed of the person I am."

Ansley looked away. "Well, that sounds all great for someone who's Ms. Self-Righteous. But I've played by all the rules for my entire life and look where it got me? It got me parentless, stuck in this small town where I'll never go anywhere. What I did wasn't working, so now I'm trying something else."

Harper didn't say anything. She'd said what she needed to say. Maybe—just maybe—Harper's words would make sense to Ansley further down the road.

She prayed that would be the case.

Ansley turned away and cast one more glance over her shoulder. "Don't hurt my brother."

"I have no intention of doing that."

But as Ansley left, Harper let the girl's warning sink in.

What would the future look like? Of course, Harper couldn't know. But would a long-term relationship between her and Luke even be possible?

She had no idea. Her life was in DC. Luke's life was here.

And, even though he was single on paper, Harper knew this town was almost like his mistress. What would it be like to deal with that fact on a day-to-day basis? Could Luke ever be a family man? Or was he like Joe, someone whose job would always be his number one priority?

These were questions Harper seriously needed to think about.

Because she hadn't come here with the intention of hurting anyone.

Chapter Twenty-Seven

HE TOOK his knife and sliced it into the flesh of the fish.

Someone had gifted him some fresh trout from a nearby stream.

He took a minute right now before all his fun began, and he allowed his knife to pierce the skin. Carefully, he cut a neat line. He made sure to go deep enough into the fish to get his desired effect.

Too shallow, and he'd have to do this all again.

That was the last thing he wanted. No, he liked to do things right the first time.

Delight rippled through him as he imagined using this same knife on his next victim.

He would follow in the tradition of his great ancestors—he just liked to add his own twist to things.

After the Pogorips had defeated their enemy, they would take the enemy's blood and smear it across their opponent's skin. It was the ultimate act of sacrifice for the warriors.

And it was the ultimate sign of defeat for the losers.

It was probably his favorite part of what he did.

Seeing the blood. Watching life drain from a person.

And then humiliating them, even after death.

A smile curled his lips.

His MO used to be at night. But time was running out, and his hunger was growing. He couldn't wait for the time to be right. Especially now that everyone was gathered at the sheriff's house.

He could never implement his plan there. There were too many people.

They thought they could slow him down. That they could stop him. That they could hurl accusations.

But he was smarter than they were.

They just didn't know it yet.

And he'd always find a way.

Tomorrow, he decided. Tomorrow he would find a way to make this happen.

He wasn't sure how yet.

He only knew he could wait no longer.

Chapter Twenty-Eight

LUKE FINISHED his last cup of coffee, ready to go back into the office. He'd only gotten a few hours of sleep last night. He'd been too busy with paperwork and talking to his contact with the Tennessee Bureau of Investigation.

Boone and Ansley had already gone to work, but Luke hoped to catch Harper before he left.

When it seemed like that might not happen, he went to the kitchen counter and started to leave her a note. Only one word in, he heard movement at the top of the stairs.

He sucked in a quick breath when he spotted Harper standing there with her tousled hair and sleepy smile.

Had there ever been a more welcoming sight? Luke couldn't imagine one. How had his feelings for this woman grown so quickly?

"Morning," she muttered, her gaze fluttering away as she pushed a hair behind her ear.

"Morning," Luke put the pen down, crumpled the paper, and tossed it into a nearby trashcan. "I was just getting ready to take off."

"Wrapping up the investigation?" Harper paused by the breakfast bar, looking like she felt out of place in the strange house.

Luke strode into the kitchen and grabbed a coffee mug, filling it for her. "That's what we're hoping. The TBI should step in from here. What are your plans?"

Would Harper leave and go back to DC? They'd never talked about the future. But the thought of this —whatever this was—ending before it had ever really begun . . . Luke didn't want to think about it.

"I think I'll head into town for the festival a little later," Harper said. "But first, I have some emails to catch up on now that all the excitement has died down."

"Sounds good. You need a ride?"

She shook her head, taking the coffee from him. "No, I've got this."

"I didn't have time to cook anything, but Boone left some apple muffins here that he got from the bakery downtown. Help yourself."

"Thank you."

He wished he had time to eat with her. But, just as the thought crossed his mind, his phone buzzed. It was Cruise.

"You need to get down to the station," Cruise said, his voice breathless and slightly panicked.

"What's going on?"

"It's Kyle. He tried to kill himself."

"How did this happen?" Luke stood outside the jail cell and stared at Kyle Bennett's lifeless figure on the floor. Paramedics surrounded him, performing CPR, but it didn't look good.

"I found a pill on the floor beside him," Cruise said.

Luke shook his head, aggravated, to say the least. "Wasn't he processed when we brought him into the station?"

Cruise swallowed hard, his face pale and his voice thin. "Yes, sir. I don't know how he got them. Maybe he hid them somewhere on his person. I don't know."

As the paramedics loaded Kyle onto a stretcher, Luke stepped back. "I need to call TBI and tell them what's going on. They were on their way to pick him up. I'll need to tell them that Kyle will be forty minutes away at the nearest hospital."

"There's one other thing," Cruise said.

"What's that?" Luke hoped it was important because this wasn't the time he wanted to hold Cruise's hand and walk him through what to do.

Luke trailed behind the paramedics. Cruise would need to go with them, to keep an eye on Kyle—not that it appeared he would be going anywhere for a long time.

"An article came out this morning about these murders."

"Okay." Luke tried to keep the impatience out of his voice.

Cruise tugged at his collar, trying to keep pace with Luke as he stepped outside near the ambulance. "It mentioned something about the photos of the cabin that were found in each crime scene."

"What? That wasn't supposed to leave our department." Another surge of agitation rushed through him. Who had leaked that information?

"I'm not sure how they found out, sir."

Luke narrowed his eyes and decided to waste no time trying to eliminate people. "You didn't say anything, did you?"

Cruise shook his head nervously, quickly. "No, sir. But I did see your friend talking to a reporter yesterday—the same one who wrote this article. His name is Bryant."

Another surge of . . . something . . . rushed through Luke. Anger? Disappointment? Both? "You mean Harper?"

"Yes, sir. Harper."

"You think she told him?"

"I have no idea."

Luke shifted, trying not to jump to any conclusions. "When did you see Harper talking to this guy?"

"Yesterday afternoon."

"She didn't know that information yet."

"That doesn't mean she didn't talk to him again later."

Luke's mind raced. Just because Cruise had seen that conversation taking place didn't mean that Harper had spilled the beans, so to speak. He'd talked to the management company. To Elmer. To Kyle.

Word could have leaked from any of those people.

But was it too much of a coincidence that the same reporter Harper had spoken with had leaked this news? Luke had wanted to keep it quiet.

Flashbacks of the Rocky Ridge Murders began to batter him.

Harper had never cared about him, had she? No, she'd just wanted information. And she'd been very skilled at finding out what she needed.

Luke had fallen for it hook, line, and sinker.

He shook his head. It was only ten o'clock, and his day just kept getting worse and worse.

Chapter Twenty-Nine

HARPER CLEANED UP FROM BREAKFAST, put her things in her car, and then stepped inside Luke's house one more time. She paused by the picture of his family on the mantel and gently picked it up.

She smiled at the faces there, but the grin quickly faded as she remembered all they'd been through. Life sure wasn't easy. But the hard times only served to make them stronger.

This family was going to be stronger than iron when all of this passed.

She put the picture down, locked the door behind her, and climbed into her car. She figured she should leave. She wouldn't be able to talk to Billy—or Kyle. The case was solved. The town was safe. Loretta wanted her back.

But Harper wanted to stay for just a while longer. Maybe it was the town. Maybe it was Luke.

She just wasn't ready to leave, though.

But as she parked in a public lot not far from the Whistling Pines Motel, her mind raced.

Why did she find it hard to believe that Kyle was Billy? Certainly there would have been something about him that triggered an internal alarm inside Harper, that made her realize that he was the same person.

But there had been nothing, not even a smidgen of recognition.

Still, Harper couldn't forget the facts. Kyle was a local who'd moved away and come back. He had Native American heritage. A picture of his cabin was found at the crime scenes, as well as the murder weapon.

Just as she stepped from her car and onto the sidewalk, something rammed into her shoulder. She glanced up as someone muttered, "Sorry."

Larry stood there, wearing his uniform, with plastic garbage bags hanging from his pockets. He looked like he was on his way into work at the Whistling Pines.

She sucked in a breath as a chill washed over her. "It's . . . it's no problem."

"Be careful here," he said, not moving. Something about the way he said it made Harper think he'd just been waiting for the opportunity to catch her alone and warn her.

The thought wasn't comforting.

"The suspect is in custody." Harper pulled her jacket closer, suddenly wishing she could get away.

Larry's gaze darkened. "Kyle Bennett isn't a killer."

Her throat tightened at the absolute certainty of his words. "Who is?"

"I have no idea. But I know this man attacked you. He's dangerous."

Harper rubbed her neck, finding it hard to breathe. Was he warning her or threatening her? "How do you know that?"

His gaze darkened. "I work maintenance. I know a lot of things that go on around here."

"I guess you do."

He pulled out his garbage bag and stepped closer to a nearby trashcan. As he did, something else tumbled from his pockets. Pills.

Strange.

He leaned down and picked them up, quickly shoving them back into his pocket.

"Be careful," he repeated.

Then he stepped away, his message delivered. Harper was sufficiently spooked now.

Someone called her name in the distance. Harper glanced behind her and saw Luke headed her way.

Instantly, she felt herself relax. Luke always seemed to make everything better.

But her shoulders tightened again when she saw his stormy expression. Gone was the warm man from this morning. What had changed?

"Did you tell your reporter friend about the picture of the cabin that was found at the crime scene?" Luke's tone sounded accusing, like he was the judge and jury, and that he'd already made his ruling.

"My friend Bryant? No. Why would I do that?"

"Didn't you talk to him yesterday?"

"Yes, but—"

"He's the one who broke the news."

Facts clicked in her mind. "Luke, I told you I wasn't like that."

His nostrils flared. "But did you mean it? Or were you just playing nice to get information?"

Harper raised her chin. He might as well have slapped her. "I can't believe you're even asking that."

"You're avoiding the question."

She let out a sharp exhale and shook her head. Disappointment bit at her. She should have known Luke was too good to be true. This instance was a prime example. He didn't believe her—just like her mom hadn't believed her all those years ago. Maybe there was something about Harper that screamed she wasn't trustworthy.

"I can't believe we're having this conversation," she finally said, her voice tight with tension "No, of course I didn't tell Bryant that. I told you I wouldn't."

Luke didn't budge. His eyes remained narrowed and his voice accusing. "Releasing information like that could put our entire investigation in jeopardy."

"You don't have to tell me that. I'm not that person." Harper shook her head. "Of course, that doesn't matter to you, does it? Your mind is already made up. You want me to be untrustworthy so you can be right—so you can hold on to your precon-ceived notion that my intentions aren't honorable."

Before Luke could say anything else, Harper turned and walked away.

How could she have been so stupid?

And why did her heart already feel broken?

That hadn't gone well.

Luke raked a hand through his hair as he stood on the sidewalk, his heart pounding as if he'd just run a marathon.

He'd been sure that Harper had been responsible.

He'd been blinded by his own assumptions. But Harper's words rang true. Maybe he was afraid—afraid of getting hurt. Of failing. Of caring too much.

He couldn't talk to Harper again now. No, she needed to cool down. And he had to deal with the situation with Kyle. The man was still alive but in crit-ical condition.

And now he'd blown it.

He took a deep breath, trying to gather himself.

He'd had to push past a crowd of reporters on his way out. The good news was that word had already spread throughout town that they'd made an arrest. The state police had arrived this morning to help out with the town's festivities.

In the distance, he heard the town carrying on as if all were normal—even though nothing felt normal.

Over in the city park, a temporary arena had been set up where the crowds sat in bleachers, cheering each other on in Highland Games type of activities—only with a fall theme. There was pumpkin tossing, and scarecrow throwing, and bobbing for apples.

Normally, those activities would bring him a sense of community and fun.

But not today.

No, there was too much on the line.

Luke's phone rang, and he recognized the number as one of his TBI agents. "Look, we just got back some evidence that I thought you'd want to know about ASAP."

"What's that?"

"The chain that was cut when the killer got into the cabin . . ."

The chain? What could they have to do with any of this? "What about the chain?"

"It turns out it was cut from the inside. I could explain the forensic process to you, but we studied the striations and—"

"I'll trust your process," Luke stopped him, willing to skip those details for now. "What did you discover?"

"The safety chain was cut from the inside out, not vice versa," he repeated.

Luke glanced around the town. "Why would the killer cut the chain after he was already inside? It doesn't make sense."

"I can't answer that. I just wanted to share the finding with you."

"Thanks," Luke muttered, ending the call.

The killer wanted to make it look like he'd broken in. But he hadn't. Somehow, he'd gotten inside and then set up the crime scene.

Luke thought about all those superstitious people in town who thought a ghost had committed these crimes. He still didn't believe in ghosts, but he was starting to understand why some people did.

Just as he ended that call, his phone rang again. It was Ms. Mary.

"Sheriff, could you come back to the station? There's something I need to tell you. I prefer to do it in person."

"Sure thing." Luke had no idea where this was going. But he wanted to find out.

Chapter Thirty

"THIS PICTURE IS NOT Kyle Bennett's cabin," Ms. Mary said, standing behind the reception counter at the sheriff's office.

Luke stared at the photo in her hands. She must have seen it on his desk. "Of course it is. We went there and saw the place for ourselves."

Ms. Mary shook her head so hard that her white hair began falling from its bun. "But you know a lot of the cabins around here look the same. There are only a limited number of builders in this area."

Luke understood what she was saying, but . . . "The windmill in the flowerbed matches."

She shook her head again. "That's because Ed Williams makes them for people at Christmastime. Plenty of people have them in their yards."

Now that she mentioned it, Luke *had* seen them before. But this photo had seemed like a slam dunk.

Luke turned toward Ms. Mary, studying her face,

which was wrinkled with wisdom and age. She wasn't one for dramatics. No, the woman had always called it like she saw it. He had no reason to think she was making this up now.

"Whose cabin is this then?" he asked. "Do you know?"

"I'm nearly certain it's Ted Munson's."

Ted Munson? Luke hadn't heard his name in years. The man had been a long-time local. He was pretty private and hadn't made a spectacle of himself around town. Since he'd stayed off radar and been a loner, Luke had very few interactions with the man. He vaguely remembered that he worked at the hardware store. "Why do you think that?"

"Easy. Ted Munson lived right beside a waterfall. Not one of the big ones, but one of the small ones that trickles down the mountain. If you look closely at this picture, you can see it."

Luke sucked in a breath at her proclamation, and he squinted at the photo. Sure enough, there was the waterfall. "What do you know about Ted Munson?"

"He died eight months ago of a heart attack."

Luke processed her words. That fit the timeline. Urgency pounded at his temples, but he needed to slow his roll and think this through. They couldn't afford to mess up again. "Did he have a son?"

"He did. His name was Steven and went to live with an out-of-state aunt when he was probably nine or ten."

His head pounded harder. What if Kyle Bennett

wasn't their guy? What if he'd been set up? "Do you remember anything about Steven?"

Ms. Mary frowned and pressed her lips together, like she didn't want the words to leave her lips. "He was a little . . . crazy, I suppose. I caught him outside church one time. He'd found a dead squirrel and . . ."

"And what?"

Ms. Mary frowned and lowered her gaze, as if trying to block out a bad memory. "He'd decided to dissect it. I tried to dismiss it as boyish curiosity. But it's always bothered me. He didn't seem bothered by death at all, like so many kids his age. Rather, he seemed to . . . well, he almost seemed to revel in it."

What if Kyle wasn't their guy? The question echoed in his mind again.

Because if Kyle wasn't their guy, then this town wasn't safe.

"Thanks, Ms. Mary." Luke stepped away, his thoughts racing.

As he walked to his office, his phone rang again. It was Boone.

"This is a bad time," Luke said, his mind racing through everything he'd just learned.

"Then I'll be quick. Have you seen Ansley?"

"She had already left for work when I got up. Why?"

"I can't get up with her." Boone's voice contained a trace of worry.

Was Ansley doing something stupid again? Drinking? Hanging out with Zach Stephens? "Did you check Hanky's?"

"Not yet. I will."

"That's where she probably is. If not, call and let me know."

"Will do. Later."

Luke changed directions and went into Dewey's office. He was officially on a short break from doing patrol, but Luke had seen him slip into his office to catch up on some paperwork during that time.

"Hey, Sheriff," Dewey said, looking up from his desk. "I was hoping to grab a moment with you."

"What's up?"

"I know Kyle is in the custody of TBI. But I found something that I think is a little weird."

"What's weird?" Luke felt like the world was turning upside down around him, and righting it again might mean sacrificing everything. He was willing to do just that. But he needed more answers first.

"I found that oil he said he was illegally disposing in the woods. Not only that, I have witnesses who place him at the location at just that time—the same time Harper was attacked."

"So you're saying Kyle isn't responsible?"

"That's what I'm saying."

Luke was beyond being surprised. The fire on the end of the dynamite was moving closer and closer to an explosion. "Dewey, I need for you to go find

Harper and keep an eye on her. If this killer is still out there, then she's a target."

His eyes widened with surprise and maybe even alarm. "What do you want me to do when I find her?"

"Stick close to her."

He shifted, quiet for a moment, before saying, "You don't think she'll think that's weird?"

Luke let out a long breath, wishing things were different. But he didn't have time to correct them now. Not yet. "Harper doesn't want to be around me right now, so it's going to have to work. Please. I have something I have to do."

"Yes, sir."

Luke needed to do some more research into Ted Munson and try to figure out who this man's son might be. Someone's life might depend on it right now.

Most likely, Harper's life.

Harper tried to push aside thoughts of her conversation with Luke. She should have known better than to wonder if there could be something between them. But she'd felt hope for the first time in a long time— and it had felt wonderful.

Hope that maybe she'd find her mythical other half, the one who made her complete. Even if Harper didn't quite believe in those things, she'd at least thought she'd found someone who could be her life partner.

She'd been foolish.

But now that there was a suspect in custody, Harper really had no reason to stay here in Fog Lake.

Except for this Fog and Hog Festival. It screamed autumn goodness. She'd enjoy it for just a while longer. She'd pick up her things from Luke's house. Find somewhere else to stay for tonight. Then first thing in the morning, she'd head back.

She might not ever have answers about why Billy had done this. She might not ever be able to talk to Kyle—or Billy. But at least she could sleep easier knowing he was behind bars.

The man had lured her here, but he hadn't gotten what he wanted. Maybe Harper had a small part in making that happen. Even if she hadn't, at least she had closure. Maybe she'd finally be able to sleep at night without those haunting memories from her childhood.

Harper's skin crawled again, and she glanced around. Crowds cheered in the background. An announcer talked about who was ahead in the pumpkin tossing competition.

Harper felt it again.

That feeling that she was being watched.

She scanned everything around her but saw no one she recognized.

Were people watching her because they thought she had something to do with this crime? Was

Danny's theory true? Had Danny spread that rumor, for that matter?

Harper had no idea.

But she had caught Danny Axton watching her. She'd also had that strange encounter with Larry. What if there was more to their stories?

"Hey, Harper," someone said from behind. "I was hoping I might run into you again."

She turned and saw Bryant Carmichael standing there.

A spike of curiosity flared inside her. They had a lot to talk about.

Chapter Thirty-One

"ARE YOU TED MUNSON'S SISTER?" Luke asked.

The woman on the other line hesitated before finally saying, "Yes, I am. I'm Ruby Jacobs."

Luke had tracked her down in Chattanooga. "Did Ted's son come to live with you when he was ten?"

"No. We weren't close. But Ted told me he put him up for adoption."

"Why is that?" Luke leaned back in his chair, squeezing and releasing the point of his ink pen in thought.

"Because he couldn't handle him anymore. He tried to institutionalize the boy, but they wouldn't admit him. Steven could be very convincing when he wanted to be."

That matched what Harper had told him about Billy.

"And that was it? You never asked any more questions?"

"Like I said, we weren't close. And I had too much going on in my life to do anything. I'm a two-time cancer survivor. All these years, I have wondered about Steven, though. I hoped he had a better life."

"What do you mean?"

"They had a strained relationship. My brother was hard on him."

"Was he abusive?"

Ruby said nothing for a moment. "I don't have any proof. It was just a feeling. Like Ted was at the end of his rope. Like he'd tried everything to get his son to behave and it hadn't worked. I think he lost his temper at times."

"Why couldn't your brother handle him anymore, Ruby?"

"He'd catch him standing over his bed at night, just staring at him."

Another checkmark.

"And you have no idea where Steven is now?" Luke clarified.

"No, I have no idea."

Luke thanked her for her time and hung up.

It definitely sounded like The Watcher was Steven Munson, also known as Billy Jennings.

Luke grabbed some yearbooks from the local schools—they kept some in their reference area at the station. He flipped through until he found a picture of Steven Munson.

The boy looked similar enough to the picture of

Billy that he'd seen. Both had lean builds, dark hair, haunted eyes.

Luke paused and checked the date on the side of the yearbook. Steven had actually been in the same class as Ansley.

Interesting. Luke would have to ask her about him whenever Ansley decided to check in.

He opened the folder where he kept all the information on this case. He kept reviewing the facts, hoping to gain fresh insight. His mind still turned over the fact that the chain on the door had been cut from the inside. Why? The detail was significant—he was sure of it.

"Hey, Cruise! Come in here," Luke called. He'd heard his deputy arrive back from the hospital. A state police officer was taking over for him, standing guard over Kyle.

Cruise stepped into his office. "Yes, sir?"

"You got the call on the night when our first victim was found, correct?"

Cruise frowned and shifted his weight. "No, sir. That was Dewey. Why?"

"It says on the police report that it was you."

Cruise shrugged, looking a touch clueless—which wasn't unusual, unfortunately. "Well, someone must have typed it in wrong. Dewey got the call, but when he arrived the woman was already dead."

The fuse continued to burn closer and closer to the dynamite. "And the second call?"

"Dewey was on call that night also."

Luke already knew the answer about the third murder. Cruise had been on call. But it had taken him a while to get there. His tire had been flat.

"Do you know when Dewey came to this area?" Luke didn't like where this was going. Yet everything was making strange sense.

"Maybe a year ago."

"Where is he living?"

"In an apartment here downtown. Why are you asking, if you don't mind?"

Luke closed his eyes—but only for a moment. But he imagined Dewey getting the call from one of the victims saying that she had seen a man lurking outside her cabin. Pictured him arriving at the crime scene. The victims would have let him in. Trusted him as an officer of the law.

And then he'd slashed their throats.

Cut the chain from the inside so no one would see him doing it and to make it look like the killer had broken in.

It would explain why there were no signs of struggle.

A sick feeling pooled in his gut.

"Have you noticed anything strange about Dewey lately?" Luke knew the two hung out on occasion.

Cruise shrugged again. "He asked to borrow a set of my class A shirts and pants a couple months ago."

Each deputy was usually given three sets of uniforms when they joined. "Why?"

"He said he was out drinking with some friends

when he stained one set of clothes. He didn't want you to know he was drinking in uniform, and he couldn't afford a new one right now.

Luke's blood felt like it was catching fire. Was that uniform stained because it had blood on it? It made sense. "Cruise, we need to find Dewey. I think he's The Watcher."

Cruise's eyes widened. "What?"

"I don't know why I didn't see it earlier. But I just sent Dewey to watch Harper." Fire burned in his blood. How could he have been so stupid? Why didn't he put the pieces together, even if only ten minutes earlier?

Now Harper's life was on the line . . . again.

"I'll look for him."

"Don't try to apprehend him alone," Luke said. "He's very dangerous. But when you have eyes on him, let me know. In the meantime, I'm going to call for backup."

Before he could, his phone rang again. It was Boone.

"This is still a bad time," Luke said.

"Luke, it's Ansley. No one has seen her. I can't find her, and I'm worried."

"Where did you get that information about the photo of the cabin?" Harper asked Bryant, trying to put her conversation with Luke out of her mind—a nearly impossible task.

"Someone sent me an anonymous email yesterday, and I decided to check into it," Bryant said. "It's a small town, so people talk. I confirmed the fact with the management company who owns the cabins. Why?"

Harper shook her head, disappointed that he'd gone to such lengths to get the information. "It wasn't supposed to be leaked yet."

He raised his chin in defiance. "Well, first one to learn it is the one to earn it. That's what I say. My editor is very happy with me right now."

"You could have compromised the investigation. It's irresponsible." Harper moved out of the way as a group of people covered in pumpkin guts walked past, laughing a little too loudly.

"People have the right to know the truth. And that's what I was doing—I was giving them the truth. Bitter much?"

"I'm not bitter. I just think there are better ways of doing things." There was so much pressure in journalism to be the one who broke news stories first, who got the interviews, who impressed editors.

Bryant's gaze darkened. "Well, if you think I'm going to get any information out of this town's sheriff, it's never going to happen. I have to go searching for answers myself. I make my own destiny."

"And it doesn't matter at what expense, does it?" Harper shook her head and turned way.

If this was what journalism was, it wasn't the career for her. She'd never been convinced it was her calling in life anyway.

Harper spotted Deputy Dewey headed her way. He glanced at Bryant for a second before looking at her again and stopping a couple feet away. "Luke sent me to get you."

"What's going on?" Just hearing Luke's name caused a pang to resound in her heart.

"I'm not sure how much I'm supposed to share." He glanced at Bryant, who got the hint and walked away with a wave.

Harper turned back to Dewey and lowered her voice. "It's not Kyle, is it? Kyle isn't Billy?"

Dewey shook his head. "No, we don't believe so. The sheriff still doesn't know who is. He wants me to get you to safety."

Harper glanced around, remembering that feeling of being watched.

Maybe the killer was still out there. Still watching. Still waiting for the right moment to strike.

Dewey escorted her into his squad car, and they took off.

When would this nightmare ever end?

Chapter Thirty-Two

LUKE CLENCHED his teeth as pressure mounted inside him.

He'd tried to call Dewey.

No answer.

He'd tried to call Harper.

No answer.

He'd tried to call Ansley.

No answer.

He needed backup to get here—now.

He couldn't sit at his desk any longer. He grabbed his hat and keys and strode from his office.

"Ms. Mary, you can lock up the office and go home."

Her eyes widened, and she looked up from the crossword puzzle she was working on. "What?"

"Trust me. Go home and stay there until I call you."

"But the festival is always so busy and—"

"Don't answer the door for anyone but me. Not Cruise. Not Dewey. No one. Understand?" The woman was a widow. She needed to be careful.

"But—"

Luke paused in front of her, not feeling like arguing. "Just promise me you'll do that. Please."

"Okay, but . . . I'm all worried now." Apprehension added more lines to her face.

"I wish I could tell you not to be worried. But I can't. This town is in trouble, and I've got to go. Say prayers. Say a lot of prayers."

"I will, Luke. I will. Stay safe."

He stormed outside and got into his SUV. He didn't know what else to do but to look for Dewey, Harper, and Ansley himself. Paperwork could wait until later.

With every moment that passed, Luke's anxiety crept higher. There was nothing about this situation that he liked. No, things were on the verge of exploding. He could feel it in his blood.

He called Cruise again.

"Did you find Dewey?" Luke asked.

"No, someone said they saw him and Harper get into his squad car about five minutes ago."

"He turned off his GPS. Any idea where he might have gone?"

"I drove by his apartment. Didn't see him there. I'll keep patrolling."

He clamped down. "You do that, Cruise. And as soon as you find him, let me know."

"Will do."

Where would Dewey have gone? Luke had no idea. but he needed to figure it out and fast.

"Where are we going?" Harper asked, looking out the window at the town as they passed.

"Luke told me to take you somewhere safe," Dewey said.

"The killer is still out there, huh?" She knew it was a repeat, but she desperately wanted to know more.

Besides, she could hardly believe the news.

Yet she could. Was it Danny Axton? Larry the Maintenance Man? Or was it someone else entirely? Someone she'd never considered as a suspect?

"It appears we got the wrong guy. It's unfortunate, especially since Kyle tried to take his own life."

"What?" She gasped. "How?"

"He overdosed in his jail cell last night."

Her pulse beat hard in her ears. "Overdosed? On pills?"

"Yep."

She remembered the pills she'd seen fall out of Larry's uniform. Was Larry behind this somehow?

"You look a little shaken," Dewey said.

She told him about her encounter with Larry that morning.

"I'll let Luke know." Dewey pulled away from

town and headed toward the mountains, toward the backroads. "In a minute."

She glanced around, noticing they were moving farther away from civilization and up into the secluded mountains. A shiver raced through her. "I'm sorry—where did you say we're going?"

"There's a cabin I figured I could take you to. Somewhere no one will find you."

Something about the way Dewey said the words sent a shiver down Harper's spine. *Where no one will find you.*

It was nothing. Everything was playing with her mind, making it hard to trust and let her guard down. What he'd meant was—where the killer wouldn't find her.

Of course.

Harper glanced over at him. The deputy had always stayed in the background whenever Luke was around, but he'd seemed reliable enough. He was quiet, but he was always there.

He'd seemed more competent than Cruise, who went pale at every mention of the killer.

Harper had a feeling Luke wouldn't have hired either man, but his father must have seen something in the two. Maybe not a lot of people applied for deputy jobs in the area. She was still learning about small-town dynamics.

"I've been meaning to ask you," Dewey said. "How can I help?"

"How can you help?" Harper repeated.

The phrase struck her as odd. Probably because her mom used to say it all the time, and the kids got in trouble when they forgot to ask. It was an expected question after dinner or other family activities where help was required.

It was just a coincidence that Dewey had used it . . . right?

She glanced at Dewey again, suddenly unable to breathe.

His eyes . . . if they were brown instead of blue. If his hair was a little darker and shorter. If he were thinner.

Before she could question herself, Dewey turned toward her, a gleam in his eyes.

And that was when Harper knew Dewey wasn't Dewey.

Dewey was Billy.

Chapter Thirty-Three

LUKE HAD SPENT the last thirty minutes searching the town, and he'd found nothing.

TBI and the state police were also helping him, in between supervising at the festival. Luke had updated them on the situation. Their agents were now searching the town also.

Boone had gotten involved. He'd helped by calling all of Ansley's friends, but no one had seen her since this morning when she arrived to work at a zipline up in the mountains.

Meanwhile, the townspeople were enjoying the Fog and Hog Festival, clueless about anything going on.

Rosie and the Men Who Stole My Land played in the background. The sun shone brightly. Main Street was closed so the crowds could fill the space.

Luke's worry only grew.

He pictured Dewey grabbing Harper.

Had he grabbed Ansley also? Was there some kind of connection there between him and Ansley since they'd been classmates? He would guess the answer was yes.

Would Dewey waste any time getting his deed done? Would he capture the two women, slice their throats, and leave their bodies for the police—or someone else—to find?

Nausea rolled in his stomach at the thought.

He couldn't let that happen.

He couldn't.

His sister didn't deserve this. She was young and stupid. But she had so much potential. She just needed to turn her life around.

And Harper . . .

Luke hadn't realized just how much Harper meant to him. Now he'd ruined it, and he might not have the chance to make things right.

He was going to head up to the old Munson cabin. It was the only thing that made sense.

Harper couldn't let Billy take her anywhere.

She wouldn't come out of it alive.

She gripped the armrest as her heart raced out of control.

"Why did you go through all this trouble?" Her voice shook as she asked the question.

Her nerves only seemed to feed his calmness, his

satisfaction, though. He smiled, not looking the least bit shaken. "For you, Harper. It's been all for you."

"I don't understand what I ever did to you." All these years, and Harper had never truly understood.

"You didn't do anything. You were just perfect. From the moment I saw you, I wanted to kill you. But you left. And I couldn't. So I tried to make ends meet by killing others. It wasn't as satisfying, though."

The utter calmness with which he said the words sent another chill up her spine.

"Why me?" She nearly croaked the sentence out.

"Because you're you. There doesn't have to be another reason."

"Billy . . ." Her voice cracked again.

Dewey had the perfect disguise. Perfect timing. Luke—if he could find her—would have trouble putting this together. By the time he did, Harper would most likely be dead.

Luke . . . she didn't want things to end the way they had between them.

Luke had reacted to her because of his past experiences. With time . . . maybe he would have seen the truth.

There had been something special between them. She'd felt it. He'd felt it.

If she died, this would just be one more thing he'd try and carry the responsibility for.

"It's okay, Harper." Billy's silky slick voice snapped her back to reality. "It will be fast."

"What will be?"

Billy grinned. "Your death."

She shivered as the situation continued to smack her in the face. Every time she let herself believe that maybe this was a nightmare, the truth came barreling down. And each time, it hurt like crazy. It sent a shock of pain through her. Nausea roiled in her gut.

"Luke will find me first," she finally said.

Harper didn't believe it—but she wanted to. If nothing else, she wanted to shake Billy's confidence.

"No, he won't. Besides, I heard he's a little upset with you."

Her cheeks burned. "You probably leaked that information yourself."

"I hate this town." Some of the smugness left his voice, replaced by bitterness.

Harper hadn't expected that. "Why?"

"It rejected me. My dad told a few people about some of my less-than-desirable actions, and the next thing I know, no one wanted to be my friend."

"He shouldn't have done that." She glanced out the window, trying to spot something familiar. But so many of these mountain roads looked the same that she couldn't tell which way was which.

"He left me, you know."

"I'm sorry. No one should do that."

"I've been planning all of this. For years. It seemed only appropriate to come back to the town that rejected me."

"Billy . . ."

"When I was eight, I had my first crush, you know."

What? Where was Billy going with this?

Harper had no choice but to listen. She had nowhere to go. The road on one side featured a steep drop-off. On the other side was a massive rock wall.

Harper licked her lips. "What happened?"

"I tried to kiss her. She laughed at me. Told everyone how stupid I was."

"That wasn't nice."

"No, it wasn't, was it? She kind of looked like you too. You've always been my type."

Harper squeezed her eyes shut, everything spinning around her. *No, don't go there. Stay in control*, she chided herself. She couldn't give into fear, though every part of her wanted to.

"You don't have to do this, Billy."

"I do. You don't even understand. It's in my blood. It's the fuse that keeps me alive. I have to do this."

Harper swallowed hard, desperate to think of a plan yet coming up blank. "You killed Shari too? She was your friend. She didn't reject you, yet you killed her. I think you're just making excuses."

"That was unfortunate. But she wasn't supposed to run into me. She could have ruined everything."

"And Tom Brock?"

"Same story. He saw me watching one of the women who died. I couldn't risk it. It was too bad, though, because he seemed like a nice man."

"And your dad?"

His gaze darkened. "Well, he deserved to die. He abandoned me on the streets to fend for myself, all because he wasn't man enough to admit that he couldn't handle me."

Harper could sense the anger rising inside of him. She had to do something. They were almost at the top of this mountain, and once they had nowhere else to go, this would all be over.

Before she could second-guess herself, Harper grabbed the wheel.

Billy muttered a curse.

The car swerved toward the edge of the mountain road. At full speed.

Billy spun the wheel to right the vehicle. But, before he could, something slammed into her head.

And everything went black.

Chapter Thirty-Four

LUKE PULLED up to the property where Steven had grown up and let out a long breath.

This cabin looked exactly like the one in the picture.

The only difference was that the place had been neglected since that photo was taken. Small trees now grew on the tin roof. The grass was overgrown. Leaves piled against the steps and flowerbeds.

But the windmill was even there, just like Ms. Mary had said.

Tension pulsated through Luke. He'd been so certain that Harper had been irresponsible and put the case in jeopardy. In truth, Luke had put Harper in danger. A surge of regret rose in him.

He'd never forgive himself if something happened to her. That was why he had to find her.

Outside, the cabin appeared empty. But that didn't mean it was.

Luke radioed the TBI. They were still five minutes out.

He couldn't wait that long.

Five minutes could mean life or death.

Carefully, Luke approached the front window. Remaining against the wall, he peered inside.

Only darkness stared back.

But he had to be sure.

He checked each window. Saw nothing.

But that wasn't enough.

Luke checked the door. It was unlocked.

Carefully, he stepped inside. The place smelled old. Musty.

And it looked empty.

Luke paused and glanced around, not ready to concede that this had been a false lead.

Was that really all there was to this house? Certainly there was a basement.

As if something had read his mind, he heard a rattle below him.

He moved aside an area rug and saw a trap door.

Slowly, he pulled it open.

Please, Lord. Help me to find Ansley and Harper. Let them be alive and well.

Harper pulled her eyes open, her head pounding with a raging headache. Darkness surrounded her.

Where was she?

Everything flooded back to her.

Dewey. Picking her up. Discovering he was Billy.

She'd grabbed the steering wheel. Blacked out.

And now this.

Where had Billy taken her?

She tried to move her hands and shove her hair from her face. But she couldn't. Something thick and bristly dug into her wrist.

An old rope, she realized.

Her hands were tied behind her back.

She sucked in a shallow breath and glanced around. It was so dark. Too dark. Impossibly dark.

She let out a scream.

"Hey, it's okay," someone said beside her. "He's not here."

Harper blinked, hoping her surroundings might come into focus. It was no use. The darkness was too overpowering.

"Who are you?" she croaked instead.

Who else would be here with her? A friend? Or a foe?

"It's me. Ansley."

Harper's heart pounded more rapidly in her ears. "Ansley? What are you doing here?"

How had Luke's sister gotten mixed up in all of this?

"I was walking out in the woods today, getting the zipline set up. Deputy Dewey came and got me. Told me Luke needed me right away. As soon as I got in the car with him, I knew something was wrong. He placed some kind of cloth over my mouth until I passed out. I woke up here."

Harper let out another moan as facts clicked together in her mind. "You were the one he tried to kiss when he was eight."

"Steven Munson," Ansley muttered. "I should have realized that's who Dewey really was. I had no interest in boys at the age, and I really had no interest in kissing one. Little did I know that Steven would hold a grudge for so long."

"Normal people don't."

"He muttered something about my dad, also."

"What about your dad?" As Harper shifted, an ache raked through her body. She closed her eyes, absorbing everything she could without seeing. The floor was cold and gritty. The area smelled dank.

Was she in a basement?

"He told me that my dad should have come to find him when his dad abandoned him," Ansley said.

Harper processed that statement, trying to get into Billy's mind. "I'm sure your dad had a good excuse."

"His father told my dad that Steven went to live with an aunt out of state. No one really thought anything about it. Truthfully, we were glad to have Steven gone. Even as a kid he gave everyone the creeps."

"Why?" Harper tugged at the rope around her wrists, but it was tied too tightly.

"The things he used to do to insects . . . I could tell you details, but you probably don't want to hear."

No, she didn't.

Instead, Harper glanced around. Her eyes still hadn't adjusted to the dark, but shadows began to appear—vague outlines of the area around her. "Any idea where we are?"

"It's too dark. I can't tell. But I'd guess we're in a basement of some type."

That matched what Harper thought also. "How long have I been down here?"

"Only about ten minutes."

Harper tried to think, to gather information, to form a plan of action. "Have you heard him walking above us? Do you know if he's close?"

"No, it's been quiet. I think he left."

Silence stretched for a moment, and Harper tried to gather her thoughts.

"He's going to kill us, isn't he?" Ansley's voice cracked.

"I . . . I don't know." But Harper knew the likelihood was yes, Billy would—unless they could stop him.

"He is going to kill us. I know he is." A small cry escaped from Ansley. "I'm not ready to die yet, Harper."

"I don't want to die either."

"No, you don't understand. I've been such a jerk lately." Ansley sniffled. "I can't let things end like this. Do you know how horrible I've been to Luke?"

Harper remembered the tension she'd heard in Luke's voice as he spoke about his family. He loved them dearly, so much that he would give up anything to help them. "Luke knows you love him. And we're going to get out of this."

"No, Steven is going to kill us. Just like he killed those other women. We're not going to stand a chance, Harper." The panic in Ansley's voice increased with each new word.

"Don't think like that. We're smart. We can think of a way out of this." The ache in Harper's head panged harder each time she moved. "We need to see what we can find in this room."

But before Harper could begin looking, the door opened.

Chapter Thirty-Five

LUKE CREPT DOWN THE STAIRS, his gun drawn, waiting for any sign of movement or life.

He shone his light on the steps in front of him. Wood stared back, each slat inviting him farther into the abyss.

As he took another step, a moist, earthy scent surrounded him.

But he saw nothing, no one—only dust particles suspended in the stream of light in front of him.

Luke continued his descent until he reached the last step. The beam of his flashlight illuminated the perimeter of the space.

Please, don't let me find Ansley and Harper here. I need them safe. Alive.

The prayer repeated in his mind.

As the place came into focus, he saw an old cellar staring back.

Luke's beam fell on three rats that climbed across some firewood against the wall.

Rats? That was what Luke had heard down here?

His heart sank.

No one was here.

If Ansley and Harper weren't at this cabin, then where would Dewey have taken them?

Luke didn't have any good ideas. But he did know that time was running out.

He had to find them.

Now.

"Now, who should I start with?" Billy smiled in front of them and turned on a flickering overhead light.

Every time it buzzed, the nausea in Harper's stomach roiled with more intensity.

Harper soaked in Billy's new appearance. Now that she knew who he was . . . she could clearly see Dewey was Billy. He'd taken out his contacts. His hair was now tousled. His demeanor had transformed from an easy-going cop to a calculated man bent on revenge.

He'd taken off his uniform and wore jeans and a T-shirt instead. A flute jutted out from his pocket, and he held a hunting knife in his hand.

Ansley gasped beside her, her gaze darting around them. "Are we . . . ?"

Billy's smile widened with satisfaction. "Perfect place, isn't it?"

Harper knew she was missing something. Ansley recognized the space where they were being kept.

"I wouldn't say that." Ansley frowned, struggling against the binds around her limbs.

"No one will find us here for quite a while. It's the last place anyone will look. Especially Luke. He'll work himself to death. Going home will be the last thing he does—out of guilt."

"We're at your house?" Harper muttered, looking at Ansley for confirmation.

How horrible . . . yet it seemed exactly like something Billy would do.

"This is my basement." Black lines of mascara streamed down Ansley's cheeks. "And he's right. Boone and Luke won't even think about coming home until I'm found."

"And then what a rude awakening that will be." Billy smiled again, the action void of any warmth.

Seeing it left Harper feeling even more frigid than before.

Harper's gaze traveled down to the knife he held in his hands. "You set up poor Kyle Bennett, didn't you? You went with Luke to question him, and that's when you planted the evidence at his place."

"Pretty clever, huh?"

Billy always thought he was clever. Harper prayed that would work to his detriment right now.

Pride comes before a fall.

"Billy, you don't have to do this." Harper knew that reasoning with him was a long shot, but she was going to try anyway. She had no other options. If she could buy time, maybe she'd think of something. Maybe help would arrive.

"I know. But I want to."

Harper quickly glanced around. Saw some gas cans. Tools. Boxes. Was there anything she could use to defend herself?

Not with these binds around her wrist.

Billy paced in front of them, flicking his knife back and forth as if it were something ordinary—like a pencil or baton. Every time he moved the weapon, Harper's stomach lurched.

That blade . . . it looked sharp. Deadly.

"Let Ansley go," Harper pleaded, rethinking how to handle this. "You have me. You don't need both of us."

"Both of you are just the icing on the cake. After you two die, no one will want to come back to this town—except for maybe those freaks who liked to be scared. The place that forgot about me will be forgotten."

And that was what it all boiled down to, wasn't it?

Billy felt like this whole area had turned a blind eye to his suffering.

"It's easier to kill when people trust you." He paced toward Harper.

Her muscles tightened, her eyes still on his knife. "Is it?"

314

"I'd say Mother will be disappointed at the news of your death, but we all know that's not true, isn't it? She can't stand you. Mostly because she loves me."

"Why would you want to hurt her like this?" *Keep him talking, Harper. Keep him talking. Buy time. Maybe someone will find us.*

"And it was so easy to make her love me. Why can't it be that easy for everyone?"

"You tricked her, Billy." Harper felt behind her and found something sharp. A discarded nail? Maybe she could use it to cut through her rope. It was worth a try.

With small motions, she began working the tip into the layers of the rope.

She missed the rope and the sharp point tore through her skin. She held back a wince, determined not to let Billy know what she was doing. And then she continued.

"You only showed Mom the best side of you," Harper continued.

"Isn't it the sign of true love when you show people who you really are and they love you anyway? Everyone I ever did that with rejected me."

Harper's heart pounded. She hated to admit it, but she felt a touch of sorrow for the man. Would his life have been different with a different family? A different upbringing? Or was it his nature that made him this way?

"How'd you fake your own death?" she asked.

He shrugged. "It wasn't hard. I found a homeless

man who matched my stats, drugged him, and set the car up for an accident. It was important that I appear dead if I wanted to get away with this. I had to set up yet another new identity. I've been Steven Munson. I've been Billy Jennings. Now I'm Deputy Dewey. I thought it had a nice ring to it."

"You attacked me in DC."

"And if you had died, maybe none of this would be happening right now. But something ignited in me that night, and I knew I needed more. I just didn't go deep enough when I cut the skin at your neck. The whole experience taught me so much."

Harper's stomach roiled again. This man . . . he had no soul, did he?

"Now you need to pay." Billy raised his knife higher. "I need to finish this. Teach you a lesson."

Harper said her prayers, unable to deny that this could be her last breath.

And as she did, her gaze fell on a sledgehammer in the distance.

If she could get her hands free . . .

If she could grab the sledge hammer . . .

If she could use it in time . . .

Then maybe they would have a chance of getting out of this alive.

Harper had no choice but to try.

Chapter Thirty-Six

AS LUKE SEARCHED THE STREETS, looking for any sign of Dewey, Ansley, or Harper, his phone rang. It was Ms. Mary.

"What's going on?" He hoped she had made it to her house safely.

"Luke, are you at home?"

His back stiffened. Of all the things she had called about at a time like this . . . "What are you talking about?"

"I drove past your house, and I saw the deputy's car there. Did I miss something?"

Luke didn't bother to ask her why it had taken her so long to get home. He was too busy focusing on what she'd said.

"When did you drive past, Ms. Mary?"

"It's been twenty minutes. I had to stop by the pharmacy and pick up my heart medicine. Figured it was a good idea with everything going on. Anyway, I keep worrying about seeing the car at your house. I've been waiting to hear something. Did you forget to call me?"

A sheriff's vehicle. At his house. Would Dewey have . . .?

Luke knew the answer. He did a U-turn, knowing exactly where he had to go. "No, Ms. Mary. You didn't miss anything. Thanks for the tip. I'm going to head there now."

He turned on his siren and rushed toward his house.

Dewey had taken Ansley and Harper there.

It would have been perfect. Going home was the last thing Luke was thinking about. Dewey would have known that.

He called for backup and sped down the road.

Help me get there in time. Please.

Any normal person who drove past wouldn't think anything about seeing a squad car there.

Anyone except Ms. Mary.

He thanked God for the provision.

Luke cut his siren well in advance of his arrival and eased off the road near his house, pulling onto a grassy area. He needed to stay quiet, and the sound of his tires on the gravel could alert Dewey to his presence. Instead, he approached the house on foot.

He drew his gun, praying about what he might see inside.

Was he too late?

He desperately hoped that wasn't the case.

Luke crept around to the back of the house and quietly unlocked the door. Watching his steps, he entered his residence.

All was quiet.

Where would Dewey have taken Ansley and Harper?

Slowly, he maneuvered through the kitchen. The living room.

Nothing. No one.

Then voices drifted up through the basement.

Dewey!

Someone pleaded with him.

Luke sucked in a breath.

Harper. That was Harper.

She was alive!

Thank You, Jesus.

He needed to proceed carefully. But the basement would make it difficult. There was only one way in.

Luke slipped through the doorway. Down one step. Down another.

He was careful not to make a sound.

He held his breath as he peered around the corner. Ansley. She sat on the floor. Against the wall.

She looked up at him, and, before Luke could stop her, her eyes widened with recognition.

No!

In an instant, Dewey realized he was there. He grabbed Ansley, and his knife went to her throat. "One step farther, and she dies."

Luke's heart rate surged with something close to

panic. He'd already lost his dad. He couldn't lose his sister too.

"Don't do that, Dewey," Luke urged him. "There's a better way."

"There's no other way," Dewey muttered, his actions controlled and purposeful. "No other way."

Luke didn't lower his gun. Not yet.

"Put it down," Dewey ordered.

"You need to let Harper and Ansley go. You know there's no good way out of this."

"You weren't supposed to find me yet. You coming here wasn't part of my plan. You can't mess this up."

At the sickly entertained sound of Dewey's voice, Luke knew beyond a shadow of doubt he was dealing with a psychopath here.

And Luke prayed again that God above would continue looking out for this situation.

Harper felt the rope at her wrist loosen.

She'd done it! The nail had frayed the rope enough for her arms to be free.

But as she stared at the scene in front of her, her heart rate quickened. How could she help right now? She wasn't certain. She only knew she couldn't sit back quietly.

Maybe Harper should have fought Billy harder from the beginning. Maybe she should have gone to more people until she found someone who believed her. Maybe she should have left her job to look for him sooner.

She couldn't change any of that.

But Harper could change things now.

Courage isn't the absence of fear.

She mentally chanted the wisdom. She was going to need it right now because her fear wanted to choke her.

She couldn't let it.

Harper glanced at Luke and realized how much she'd come to care about him. Realized how much she wanted to explore their relationship.

First, she had to stop Billy.

Before she could second-guess herself, she sprang from the floor. In one quick movement, she grabbed the sledgehammer and raised it.

Billy looked at her, his eyes wide.

His hand flexed around the knife.

No!

Harper swung the tool until it slammed into the side of Billy's head.

Billy let out a groan and fell to the ground. The knife flew from his hand.

Ansley darted away from his grasp and collapsed near the wall.

But she was okay. She was alive.

Quickly, Harper grabbed the knife, just in case Billy regained his senses.

Luke rushed downstairs, cuffs in hand. As Billy

moaned, Luke turned him over and secured his hands.

Billy wouldn't be hurting anyone else ever again.

TBI agents flooded into the space.

Harper knew everything was going to be okay.

She collapsed beside Ansley, her legs no longer able to hold her up. She heaved in deep gulps of air, replaying what had happened. Wondering if this was a dream.

It wasn't.

Luke knelt in front of them and pulled Ansley and Harper into his arms.

"I'm so glad you're both okay," he muttered. "I can't tell you how happy I am right now."

Harper closed her eyes. Happy didn't even begin to describe her relief.

For the first time in years, she felt like she could breathe again.

———

Harper stood in the background, watching as TBI agents took over the crime scene. Luke would be occupied helping them for a while. In the meantime, she and Ansley sat in Luke's SUV outside and drank coffee under Cruise's supervision. He'd been ordered not to let them out of his sight for any reason. Even though Billy was in custody, it was just a precaution—one that Harper was grateful for.

"I like you." Ansley's voice cut through the silence.

Harper glanced at the woman beside her. Dirt smudged her face, her hair was tousled, and her eyes were bloodshot. Somehow, beneath the tough exterior Ansley wore, a little girl was buried deep inside. Harper could see the woman's hurts right now as clearly as she could see the blanket over her shoulders.

"Thank you," Harper finally responded, uncertain what else to say.

"I think you'd be good for my brother."

Harper looked out the window at Luke's house for a moment and drew in a breath as Ansley's words washed over her. "Your brother doesn't want anything to do with me right now. He thinks I leaked information to the press."

"He'll get over it. Don't give up on him, Harper. He needs someone like you in his life. And I don't know you that well, but I have a feeling that you need someone like Luke in your life also."

Something about Ansley's words caused an ache to form in Harper's heart. Or maybe the ache had always been there, she'd just now realized it.

Ansley was right. Harper did need someone like Luke. Someone was who loyal. Protective. Who wouldn't give up on her.

She was making the best of what life had handed her, but she didn't love being a reporter in DC. What she really wanted was a place to belong. Could that place be Fog Lake? Could that person be Luke?

The man had risked his own life to save her. He'd shown humility when he apologized for his misconceptions about her. He'd shown vulnerability when he'd opened up about his struggles. He was loyal to his family, sacrificing everything to try and help them.

He was pretty much everything Harper could want in a man . . . and more.

Harper glanced outside. It had started to rain, a steady drip that reminded her of autumn and made her want a fireplace to warm up in front of.

She thought about the festival downtown. Had the dampness distracted the crowds there?

She doubted it. Those crowds were determined to enjoy this town.

Which made Harper believe that this town would survive. It had a fighting spirit. A *resilient* spirit.

One person couldn't ruin what decades had developed.

Luke knocked at the window, and Harper opened the door just a crack, trying to keep the rain out.

"Hey, can I talk to you a minute?" Luke's voice sounded subdued and husky.

Harper's breath caught as she realized the implications of his question. This conversation would determine their future—or lack thereof. "Sure."

Luke took Harper's hand and tugged her out. He didn't let go of her until they were beneath his porch roof, tucked in the corner away from the agents who were coming and going.

"How are you?" He studied her face without attempting to hide it. His gaze was filled with worry . . . and maybe apology.

"I'm okay. As well as can be expected." Harper shivered as she remembered tonight's events. If just one thing had happened differently, she could be dead right now. This could be a very different scene.

And she was eternally grateful for the hope of tomorrow.

"Harper . . ." Luke looked into the distance, and she knew he was struggling to find the right words.

"It's okay." Harper squeezed his arm.

"What's okay?" he asked.

"I forgive you for jumping to conclusions about me leaking that information to the press. I didn't do it."

"I realize that." Luke lowered his gaze. "And I am sorry. When I heard you were missing . . . I knew that, even if you had done it, it wouldn't change the way I feel about you."

"I wouldn't betray your trust like that."

"I know." His voice cracked, and he ran a hand over his face. "I know. Sometimes fear propels our actions more than it should."

"I understand that. I battle with fear all the time. Fear that I didn't do the right thing. That I'll be rejected again. That I can't make it on my own."

"I guess we all have a little of that apprehension buried deep down inside us," Luke murmured.

"As long as we don't let it win, we'll be okay, right?"

Harper stepped into his arms and nestled there. It felt good to have Luke close. To know that Billy really was locked up this time. Even the rain seemed to sense that this area needed a touch of comfort, and the steady drops did just that. Their rhythm was serene and cozy as Harper listened to it hit the tin roof above her.

"I don't know what the future holds, Harper," he whispered into her hair. "I know your life is back in DC."

"And I know your life is here. But we're going to figure it out. I know we will."

Luke's hands cupped her face. That same unseen force seemed to surround them, pulling them closer.

Their lips met, and for a moment—and just a moment—all of Harper's worries disappeared.

Epilogue

TWO MONTHS LATER

"I'VE ALWAYS WANTED to celebrate Christmas in the mountains," Harper said, pulling her sweater closer.

She stood on a dock overlooking Fog Lake, and Luke sat behind her in a wooden chair.

This wasn't just any dock.

No, this was the dock that Luke had built by the lake below his family's house. He'd added a pergola and some built-in benches. He completed the whole project with a plaque, dedicating the area to his father.

It was perfect.

Harper glanced around, marveling at the snow-covered treetops. From where she stood, she spotted numerous cabins nestled on the mountainside. Many had strung Christmas lights around their edges, making the whole lake look magical. She knew that not far behind her, in the downtown area, there were Christmas trees, festive lights, and decorative displays.

There would be a lot of people coming to this area to do the very thing she was doing: spending Christmas in the beautiful, mysterious Smokies.

Luke tugged at her hand and pulled her toward him. Harper somehow landed in his lap, and her arms somehow ended up wrapped around his neck, as if she'd done it a million times before. And she had. Maybe not a million times, but she was working on it.

"I'm glad you're here, Harper," he murmured. "Really glad."

"I couldn't ask for a better town."

"Oh, is it the town that's keeping you here?" he teased.

She shrugged. "Well, what else would it be?"

He nudged her closer. "Oh, I don't know."

"I did hear that there's a smokin' hot sheriff in these parts."

"Smokin' hot?"

Harper shrugged again. "That's what a group of tourists said when they came into the coffee shop the other day. They said he should be added to the list of attractions in the area, and he was one more reason to visit Fog Lake. He might just single-handedly save the town, after all."

A deep chuckle rose inside him. "Okay, well, as long as groups of tourists think that, I guess I'm okay."

Harper's chuckles died as her hands caressed the

side of his face. "No, it's absolutely all you that keeps me here."

"I'm glad to hear that." His voice sounded husky with emotion, and his eyes glowed with unmistakable warmth.

Harper leaned toward Luke, and their lips met briefly before she cuddled back against him to enjoy the scene around them.

Somehow, everything was starting to feel normal.

Billy—Steven Munson —was behind bars. And he'd be there the rest of his life.

Kyle had woken up from his overdose. He was doing better, and he was back to working at the diner and acting like himself.

Billy must have slipped those pills into Kyle's pocket after he'd been processed down at the station. He hadn't owned up to it, but everyone knew that was the most likely scenario.

The pills that had fallen out of Larry's pocket? Apparently, they were for heartburn. Harper had learned that tidbit about the man after talking to him at the coffee shop one day. He wasn't actually as creepy as she'd originally thought.

Ansley had been sober for two months. She'd been scared straight, as they said.

Boone was enjoying life, as normal.

And Harper . . . she'd found an apartment to rent for the time being. And she was putting her writing skills to good use since she'd taken a job helping with marketing for the town. She was working hard to continue to bring tourism to the area and keep people's lights on here, so to speak. It was surprisingly fulfilling and a welcome break from politics.

There truly was no place she'd rather be than here in Fog Lake with Luke.

"Harper?" Luke murmured.

"Yes." She still rested her head against his chest, her eyes closed.

"Harper," he repeated.

She heard the urgency in his voice and opened her eyes. She pushed herself up, instantly missing his warmth. "Yes?"

He extended his arm and raised his eyebrows. Her gaze traveled to his hand, where he held a . . . ring.

She gasped as the details came into focus. "Is that . . .?"

A grin spread across Luke's face, and those dimples appeared. "Harper Jennings, you've reminded me that there's another side of life—a side that doesn't require working too much and being saddled with guilt. You've reminded me how important it is to fight for what you believe in. For *who* you believe in."

Tears welled in her eyes.

"I know some people might say this is too soon, but Harper, I don't want to wait any longer. Will you marry me?"

"Marry you?" The tears came out harder. This was really happening. Luke was proposing. "Yes! Yes, I'll marry you!"

He chuckled as he slipped the ring on her finger and planted a long kiss on her lips.

"I didn't plan on doing it this way. I was going to be more extravagant."

Harper stared at the ring. "No, this is perfect. Just perfect, Luke."

"Yes, you are."

She felt her cheeks heat as she turned back to him, her heart nearly exploding with joy. There was so much she could say. But instead, she kissed Luke again.

As she hoped she would be doing for a long, long time.

Also by Christy Barritt:

You also might enjoy: Lantern Beach
Mysteries

Hidden Currents

You can take the detective out of the investigation, but you can't take the investigator out of the detective. A notorious gang puts a bounty on Detective Cady Matthews's head after she takes down their leader, leaving her no choice but to hide until she can testify at trial. But her temporary home across the country on a remote North Carolina island isn't as peaceful as she initially thinks. Living under the new identity of Cassidy Livingston, she struggles to keep her investigative skills tucked away, especially after a body washes ashore. When local police bungle the murder investigation, she can't resist stepping in. But Cassidy is supposed to be keeping a low profile. One wrong move could lead to both her discovery and her demise. Can she bring justice to the island . . . or will the hidden currents surrounding her pull her under for good?

Flood Watch

The tide is high, and so is the danger on Lantern Beach. Still in hiding after infiltrating a dangerous gang, Cassidy Livingston just has to make it a few more months before she can testify at trial and resume her old life. But trouble keeps finding her, and Cassidy is pulled into a local investigation after a man mysteriously disappears from the island she now calls home. A recurring nightmare from her time undercover only muddies things, as does a visit from the parents of her handsome ex-Navy SEAL neighbor. When a friend's life is threatened, Cassidy must make choices that put her on the verge of blowing her cover. With a flood watch on her emotions and her life in a tangle, will Cassidy find the truth? Or will her past finally drown her?

Storm Surge

A storm is brewing hundreds of miles away, but its effects are devastating even from afar. Laid-back, loose, and light: that's Cassidy Livingston's new motto. But when a makeshift boat with a bloody cloth inside washes ashore near her oceanfront home, her detective instincts shift into gear . . . again. Seeking clues isn't the only thing on her mind—romance is heating up with next-door neighbor and former Navy SEAL Ty Chambers as well. Her heart wants the love and stability she's longed for her entire life. But her hidden identity only leads to a tidal wave of turbulence. As more answers emerge about the boat, the danger around her rises, creating a treacherous swell that threatens to reveal her past. Can Cassidy mind her own business, or will the storm surge of violence and corruption that has washed ashore on Lantern Beach leave her life in wreckage?

Dangerous Waters

Danger lurks on the horizon, leaving only two choices: find shelter or flee. Cassidy Livingston's new identity has begun to feel as comfortable as her favorite sweater. She's been tucked away on Lantern Beach for weeks, waiting to testify against a deadly gang, and is settling in to a new life she wants to last forever. When she thinks she spots someone malevolent from her past, panic swells inside her. If an enemy has found her, Cassidy won't be the only one who's a target. Everyone she's come to love will also be at risk. Dangerous waters threaten to pull her into an overpowering chasm she may never escape. Can Cassidy survive what lies ahead? Or has the tide fatally turned against her?

Perilous Riptide

Just when the current seems safer, an unseen danger emerges and threatens to destroy everything. When Cassidy Livingston finds a journal hidden deep in the recesses of her ice cream truck, her curiosity kicks into high gear. Islanders suspect that Elsa, the journal's owner, didn't die accidentally. Her final entry indicates their suspicions might be correct and that what Elsa observed on her final night may have led to her demise. Against the advice of Ty Chambers, her former Navy SEAL boyfriend, Cassidy taps into her detective skills and hunts for answers. But her search only leads to a skeletal body and trouble for both of them. As helplessness threatens to drown her, Cassidy is desperate to turn back time. Can Cassidy find what she needs to navigate the perilous situation? Or will the riptide surrounding her threaten everyone and everything Cassidy loves?

Deadly Undertow

The current's fatal pull is powerful, but so is one detective's will to live. When someone from Cassidy Livingston's past shows up on Lantern Beach and warns her of impending peril, opposing currents collide, threatening to drag her under. Running would be easy. But leaving would break her heart. Cassidy must decipher between the truth and lies, between reality and deception. Even more importantly, she must decide whom to trust and whom to fear. Her life depends on it. As danger rises and answers surface, everything Cassidy thought she knew is tested. In order to survive, Cassidy must take drastic measures and end the battle against the ruthless gang DH-7 once and for all. But if her final mission fails, the consequences will be as deadly as the raging undertow.

Squeaky Clean Mysteries

On her way to completing a degree in forensic science, Gabby St. Claire drops out of school and starts her own crime-scene cleaning business. When a routine cleaning job uncovers a murder weapon the police overlooked, she realizes that the wrong person is in jail. She also realizes that crime scene cleaning might be the perfect career for utilizing her investigative skills.

Holly Anna Paladin Mysteries:

When Holly Anna Paladin is given a year to live, she embraces her final days doing what she loves most—random acts of kindness. But when one of her extreme good deeds goes horribly wrong, implicating Holly in a string of murders, Holly is suddenly in a different kind of fight for her life. She knows one thing for sure: she only has a short amount of time to make a difference. And if helping the people she cares about puts her in danger, it's a risk worth taking.

The Worst Detective Ever:

I'm not really a private detective. I just play one on TV.

Joey Darling, better known to the world as Raven Remington, detective extraordinaire, is trying to separate herself from her invincible alter ego. She played the spunky character for five years on the hit TV show *Relentless*, which catapulted her to fame and into the role of Hollywood's sweetheart. When her marriage falls apart, her finances dwindle to nothing, and her father disappears, Joey finds herself on the Outer Banks of North Carolina, trying to piece together her life away from the limelight. But as people continually mistake her for the character she played on TV, she's tasked with solving real life crimes . . . even though she's terrible at it.

#1 Ready to Fumble

About the Author

USA Today has called Christy Barritt's books "scary, funny, passionate, and quirky."

Christy writes both mystery and romantic suspense novels that are clean with underlying messages of faith. Her books have won the Daphne du Maurier Award for Excellence in Suspense and Mystery, have been twice nominated for the Romantic Times Reviewers' Choice Award, and have finaled for both a Carol Award and Foreword Magazine's Book of the Year.

She is married to her Prince Charming, a man who thinks she's hilarious—but only when she's not trying to be. Christy is a self-proclaimed klutz, an avid music lover who's known for spontaneously bursting into song, and a road trip aficionado.

When she's not working or spending time with her family, she enjoys singing, playing the guitar, and exploring small, unsuspecting towns where people have no idea how accident-prone she is.

Find Christy online at:
   www.christybarritt.com
   www.facebook.com/christybarritt
   www.twitter.com/cbarritt

Sign up for Christy's newsletter to get information on all of her latest releases here: **www.christybarritt.com/newsletter-sign-up/**

If you enjoyed this book, please consider leaving a review.

Buddy 12/15/18

Made in the USA
Columbia, SC
24 November 2018